ML NYSTROM

———— HOT TREE PUBLISHING ————

Mute © 2018 by ML Nystrom

All rights reserved. No part of this book may be used or reproduced in any written, electronic, recorded, or photocopied format without the express permission from the author or publisher as allowed under the terms and conditions with which it was purchased or as strictly permitted by applicable copyright law. Any unauthorized distribution, circulation or use of this text may be a direct infringement of the author's rights, and those responsible may be liable in law accordingly. Thank you for respecting the work of this author.

Mute is a work of fiction. All names, characters, events and places found therein are either from the author's imagination or used fictitiously. Any similarity to persons alive or dead, actual events, locations, or organizations is entirely coincidental and not intended by the author.

For information, contact the publisher, Hot Tree Publishing.

WWW.HOTTREEPUBLISHING.COM

EDITING: HOT TREE EDITING
COVER DESIGNER: CLAIRE SMITH
FORMATTING: RMGRAPHX

ISBN: 978-1-925655-60-5

10 9 8 7 6 5 4 3 2 1

This book is dedicated to all those who have dreams
they want to explore someday.
I hope all your somedays turn into todays.

CHAPTER ONE

The gas pump finally clicked off, leaving me with a grand total of ninety-two cents in my checking account. It was nerve-racking, but I had food in the refrigerator at my apartment and now a full tank of gas. My last paycheck from the library was coming on Friday, three days from now, and I was starting a new job tonight bartending—or at least the training. I just prayed that no crisis came up between now and the weekend. I had a small cash stash in my underwear drawer for emergencies, which consisted of a couple twenties, but that was it. It was a miracle that earlier today I was offered a job that should pay enough to cover all my bills and allow me to work around my class schedule.

My Ford Taurus was over twenty years old, made some time in the early nineties. I was hoping it would last until I graduated and got a real job so I could buy something better. That most likely wouldn't happen, as the check engine light that had been flashing at me from time to time was now constantly blinking. *Just one more month, Fred*, I chanted in my mind. *Just one more month and I can afford to get you fixed.* I had just enough time before my new job started to run back to the small apartment I shared with another student, and as it seemed more and more lately, her boyfriend too.

I reached the apartment blocks that were set above some downtown businesses, and used my key to get in the street door. Attending a community college meant there were no dorms, so we had to take what housing we could get. The neighborhood wasn't the best, and our apartment wasn't fancy by any means, but as broke college students, it was what we could afford. As long as it had running water and heat, I was good. I wanted to talk with my "roommates" about how Sheila's boyfriend should chip in with either rent or at least cleaning the apartment since he was there so often, eating our food and using up the hot water. But I never did. At five foot four, I wasn't the tallest girl in the world, but I also wasn't categorized as short either. I'd always hated confrontation, always blending into the background. There was nothing special to set me apart from the crowd. I was smart enough, but not brilliant; I was pretty enough, but not striking or memorable; and I didn't have any talents that made me stand out in a crowd. I was solidly average and mostly invisible. I preferred it that way. If you weren't seen, then you couldn't be hurt, right?

Neither Sheila nor Chip were around, so I had the place to myself for a change. I took just enough time in the apartment to brush out and rake back the mass of shoulder-length light brown hair on my head into its standard ponytail. Normally I would braid it to try and tame the wild fly-aways, but I wanted to get to my new job as quick as I could. I changed shirts and dusted a little powder across my nose, and headed out the door.

My faithful Fred coughed and sputtered in the parking lot just behind the bar, the bright red check engine light glaring at me. If I wasn't so broke, I would've taken it to the shop this morning before classes, but tuition was due, and I was so close to finally finishing nursing school. At twenty-six years old, I was one of the oldest students in the nursing program, but that was just the way life happened for me. I didn't have real parents. Never met the ones that made me, nor did I want to know anything about them. I had some nice and some not-so-nice foster parents during my years of being shuffled around from house to house and city to city in the state of North Carolina. Either way, I was out of the system at eighteen and had to make my own way, which was damn near impossible as a teenager with no money and an average high school education. It's also hard to get student loans with no credit score or cosigners, and honestly, I didn't want to graduate with a huge mountain of debt putting me in a financial hole that would take decades to dig out of. With no real skills and a tight job market, my first job was at a fast food place near the town where my last foster home had been. I flipped burgers, lived with another girl in a small one-bedroom apartment, and saved as much as I could. I managed to enroll in the nursing program at the local community college, taking one class at a time, sometimes two if I could afford it. I occasionally had to skip a semester if money was too tight, but I was determined to finish this and get some security in my life. I moved to Bryson City and took a part-time job at the library to be closer to the campus and the hospital. One more semester, some intern practicum, and I would finally be done.

My biggest problem had been finding a new job before my miracle occurred earlier today. Paying tuition had wiped me out, and the position at the library was only for the summer. I was getting a little desperate with my checking account down to double digits and no savings to speak of.

I met Betsey at the library weeks ago when she brought her grandkids in for the afternoon story time hour. Every Wednesday morning at ten she walked in the double doors wearing her high-heeled boots, even in the summer. You'd never know she was a grandmother by the way she looked and dressed in a biker babe uniform of tight jeans, colorful printed T-shirts, and a jacket that had "Property of Brick" sewn into the back. Somehow she could pull it off and not look tacky or like she was trying to hide her age. Her two grandkids were Michelle, who just turned five and would be starting kindergarten next week, and Cody, who was almost three. Both kids were beautifully behaved, always sitting quietly while I read the story, and usually had questions for me after. Earlier today I read a classic fairy tale to the group of kids, and Michelle piped up right after the story ended. I smiled as I recalled the memory and how it led me to this job.

"Why didn't Rapunzel just cut her own hair off?" Michelle asked. "She could do her own rope and get away instead of waiting for the prince."

I looked in her curious blue eyes and gave her an answer. "Maybe she didn't have any scissors that could cut her hair."

"But the story said she had to do all the sewing, so she had to have had a pair of scissors around somewhere. Remember? The witch grabbed them outta the basket."

I laughed and touched her silky blonde hair. "You know what? You're right. That's called a plot hole, and I guess the writer didn't catch it, but you did. That's really smart! Maybe you can rewrite the story someday so it makes better sense and Rapunzel can take care of herself better."

She screwed up her face and Cody did the same, happy to copy whatever his big sister did.

"I don't ever want to wait for a prince to come get me. I'll get out of the tower, get on my Harley, and drive off."

"Great idea!" I laughed because she was right. "Okay, kids, time for snack and craft." She was right indeed, as her family were lifetime members of a local motorcycle club, the Dragon Runners. Her grandmother, Betsey, was one of the "old ladies" in the MC and owner of the River's Edge Bar located just outside town on the Tuckasegee River. Her father was Blue, Betsey's son, who oddly enough was not an active member of the MC, but a town deputy. How that worked out, I had no idea. I didn't know a lot about them as a group, but it was hard to avoid them, as they had a number of businesses around the town and many people knew enough to talk about them. I'd seen some of the members around town wearing their leather cuts with a twisting, green-fire-breathing dragon on the back. I'd never heard of them being a bad bunch, just a little rowdy, but they were still a motorcycle club, and most people in the town held them in respect along with a little fear.

"You're real good with kids, Katrina," Betsey said that afternoon in her country twang. "Cody and Shells love coming here and listening to your stories. Them voices you do? That's their favorite part. Cody loved them 'Hank the Cow Dog' books so much I had to get some for my house. He tells me 'Maw-maw, you don't do it right! Do it like Kat at the library.'"

"Thanks," I replied, handing a small cup of apple juice to one of the kids. "I'm going to miss seeing them here."

"You going somewhere?" she asked, her perfectly plucked eyebrows rising in a painted arc.

"Not exactly. Summer reading groups are over, so the library doesn't need me here anymore. I've got to find a different job anyway, someplace I can work at nights." I wiped up a spill and scooped cookie crumbs into my hand to dump into the trash can. No matter how careful I was about napkins and serving, kids were messy.

"That's a shame! How come?"

"I'm starting my last set of fall classes next week, and then I have practicum hours to fill in the spring. My days will be full, and night work is all I'll be able to do. I can finally see the end of the tunnel for school, but I still need to pay rent and bills. I'll hit up the diners this afternoon and see what I can find. Hopefully something will be available, and quick."

Her whole body perked up. "You done any waitressing or bartending?"

MUTE

I paused from straightening the tiny kid-sized chairs. I'd been taught a long time ago not to get my hopes up too high. Most of the time something would come along and smack them back down again.

"Yes, I did a bit earlier this summer at the Cork and Bean restaurant. Mostly kitchen help, but I did serve when they were shorthanded, and I learned enough to fill in at the bar from time to time. I was only extra help, and they didn't need me long-term."

"Well then, I need the help and I need it now," she stated bluntly. "I got a couple girls doing summer work, but they's getting ready to go back to school themselves. If they'd be stickin' around I'd probably fire them anyways; lately they work only when they want to and not when I need 'em. Just because summer is endin' don't mean my bar is closin'. We stay hoppin' the whole year! Only season change is I close up at midnight in the winter months 'stead of one o'clock in the mornin'. You need a job? You'll come work for me, startin' tonight if you can," she announced decisively, her dyed red hair bouncing as she nodded. "It's a bar owned by the Runners, but I run the place with a coupla the boys helpin' out. The boys are there a lot and sometimes get rowdy, but I'll be there with you. Bet the pay rate is higher than here. There's hourly, plus you'll get a share of the jar tips when you're behind the bar and whatever tips you get if you're on the floor. You can work whatever nights are best for you and as many as you need."

I stared at her as she rapid-fired the job offer at me. I was surprised to say the least at Betsey's generous offer.

7

ML Nystrom

A job exactly what I needed and when I needed it the most? This kind of thing never happened to me, and I was a bit intimidated. I was used to struggling for what I needed, and this woman was offering me what amounted to a miracle. She barely knew me and was willing to take a chance on me. It was a humbling thought, but a scary one as well.

"Are you sure you want to hire me? What if I mess things up? Don't you want to interview me?"

She blew out a noisy breath, and flipped her hand up. Her long, pointed nails were coated in red polish and looked rather lethal. I got the impression not many people messed with her.

"It ain't that hard. You pour a lot of beer, a lot of shots, do some waitressin' as needed, and help keep things clean. I got a recipe book with t'other stuff, but there ain't too many sissy drinks that get served in a biker bar, 'specially now that most the tourists are heading home. The boys come in shifts most of the time to hang out and be seen. Usually they pick up women to take up to the Lair for the night, but anything goes down at the bar, they handle it so it's a safe place. My partner and bouncer is there every night seeing to business, and protectin' the club and anyone I say needs protectin'. Everythin' else, I'll handle."

She squinted at me, and I swear she was preparing to spout fire.

"You gotta problem with bikers in an MC?" she growled low. It should've scared me, but oddly enough, it didn't. Still, I answered carefully. My gut was churning at the thought of working at the River's Edge Bar, but I really needed this to work out.

"No, ma'am, I don't. I've never been around a biker club, but I've seen the Runners around town. I've taken my car to their... I mean... y'all's garage before. Just hardworking people is all I see." My heart beat nervously. *Don't screw this up, Kat! This could be the break you need!*

Betsey smiled, and clapped her hands.

"Oh Lord have mercy, girl, I ain't no ma'am! Call me Betsey, and you'll do just fine! Come on out sometime around seven o'clock tonight and I'll get you started."

That was my first introduction to the world of the Dragon Runners, and I had no idea what to expect.

CHAPTER TWO

River's Edge Bar was one of several holdings owned by the Dragon Runners. The club had quite a number of businesses in the town and surrounding area. They owned this bar, a custom bike and car garage, a pawnshop, and four or five campgrounds scattered through the Great Smoky Mountains. I'd never heard of any MC owning campgrounds, but I was sure there were many other things I'd never heard of as well. I knew these were the legitimate businesses of the club, and from what I could tell, profitable ones as well. I'd lived in the area long enough to have heard rumors of some illegal stuff that the club used to dabble in, but that had all changed when Betsey's husband, Brick, had taken over as president. The MC had a tough reputation still, and many of the townsfolk regarded them as a lawless group, but from the outside looking in, the club had gone completely legit and had a great income.

I didn't know the members personally, just through glimpses of their familiar dragon logo and by town talk.

What I'd heard from other people about the club was if you didn't mess with them, they wouldn't mess with you. Some even said they were a big help to the economy and kept the town safer than the local police. I would simply keep my head down, my mouth shut, and just do my job. My habit for years was to stay invisible, and I intended to do just that.

Across the main road, in front of the bar, was the entrance to the Dragon Runners' private compound, affectionately called the "Lair." It was not much more than a dirt road with a Keep Out sign posted. It wound up the small mountain, disappearing into the wooded area on top. I knew of the Lair and what it was, but I'd never laid eyes on it and probably never would. Entrance to the clubhouse was by invitation only, and there was no situation I could think of that would ever get me an invite.

The bar looked busy, even for a Tuesday night. A row of motorcycles decorated the front of the log cabin-style building. Everything inside was rustic, clean and inviting, definitely not what I thought a biker bar would look or feel like, but this was the one open to the public. The floors were a tightly fit polished wood, and when I first entered the building, I saw the massive wood bar with its mirror wall and floor-to-ceiling shelves full of liquor bottles. The stools in front of the bar looked more like chainsaw art than stools. They were carved to look like the back end of a horse; each one was different but functional. The floor was filled with square wood tables and wood chairs that had a rustic, homemade look. To the right of the bar was a raised area that held several pool tables and a couple of old video game consoles. The left of the bar opened up into a bigger area that had another raised area used for local bands, and a small dance floor. There were several flat-screen TVs on the walls, all showing different sports. On the brief tour Betsey gave me, I saw a couple of "members only" rooms were in the back as well as the storage room, large kitchen, and small office.

Some Dragon Runners were there. It seemed the bar was a stopping and gathering place for the bikers before heading to the private compound. All of them had nicknames that later I found out were called road names. Betsey introduced me to her husband, the club president, Brick. Cutter and Taz were sitting with him, and I got the impression they were also in charge of running the club, maybe like management. Taz looked like he was similar in age to Brick, somewhere in his late fifties or early sixties. Cutter was a bit younger, maybe in his late forties. Even though they were friendly, they exuded an aura of dominant male power. I was intimidated, but for some reason, not really scared of them. It was more like a sense of protection for those included in their circle. I didn't think they were a danger to me but I didn't want any of them to get mad at me either. I also met Stud, one of the younger members, in his early thirties. It was hard for me to meet his blue eyes as he was model gorgeous, and that kind of man was really intimidating to me. He was friendly and outgoing, greeting me as a member of the family even though I was just the hired help. Nonetheless, there was a do-not-fuck-with-this-club vibe in the air.

I was behind the bar, pulling another beer from the

tap for Stud, when the room seemed to go still. I looked up and saw another club member in the doorway, one I'd not met yet. He wasn't just big, he was BIG. He wore a tight black tank under his cut that showed off thick, hard arms covered in tribal tattoos, black jeans that molded to his strong, muscular thighs, and heavy black biker boots. He had a striking and strong presence, and I felt my gut tighten in startled reaction. He wore his black hair long and loose, waving back from his face, and looked like he might have some Native American blood, probably Cherokee as there was a reservation nearby. When he walked in the bar, I swear the air temperature dropped. This guy's aura said he would fuck you up if you dared get out of line. His eyes were piercing, could freeze you to the spot in an instant. He was a wall, unsmiling, expressionless.

I swallowed the sudden fear that clogged my throat. *Invisible, I'm invisible. He doesn't really see me.*

"What's up, Mute?" Stud bellowed.

Mute didn't say anything, but jerked his head in a nod and sat at the end of the bar. He leaned on his elbows and thumped the counter twice with his thick knuckles. I hesitated, and then hurried over to take his order. This was one biker I did not want to piss off.

"Um... what can I get you?" My voice came out soft and squeaky. I noticed his left ear was pierced with a single silver hoop, and he had a thick silver woven chain around his neck, as well as a leather choker, a couple of matching bracelets, and multiple silver rings on his fingers.

He frowned. The thick black mustache that framed

13

his mouth and chin contracted menacingly as his full lips tightened. His brows arced together in irritation, making hard lines on his forehead. His black eyes bored into mine with an unspoken threat. He stood up and thumped again.

I froze, unable to break away from his penetrating gaze. I now knew firsthand what deer-in-headlights syndrome felt like. I could feel my knees starting to shake as fight or flight set in. I sputtered.

"Um… I… um…."

His face went even darker, and he seemed to swell bigger in rage, reminding me of the Hulk. My eyes widened and I held my breath. Definitely flight. As soon as possible!

"I got you, Mute," Betsey trilled behind me. She placed a large white mug filled with black coffee in front of him. He nodded to her and lifted it to his lips. He shrank back down to his regular human size, which was only a little less threatening.

"Come here for a minute, Kat."

Betsey moved over to the other side of the long bar, wiping its gleaming surface as she went. The woman was constantly moving, full of energy, talking and laughing with a smile on her face as she moved around. Right now, she was not smiling.

"Mute don't talk. At all. Underneath that choker is a scar from a knife fight years ago, before he joined the club. I ain't gonna tell you the whole story, as there's parts of it I don't know. We ain't exactly strict on it, but most club business ain't something the women get involved in. Not even old ladies."

She dropped the cleaning rag on the lower counter and turned to face me. Despite saying she wouldn't tell me the whole story, she proceeded to do just that.

"What I do know is he was jumped by three men who beat him up badly, cut his throat, and left him to die. I don't know why it happened, just that he should have died from it. He held his throat together and by pure grit and guts managed to get hisself to the hospital. By some miracle, the doctors were able to stitch him back up and he survived, but his voice didn't. His vocal chords were cut or got tore up too much to ever heal right. When he got outta the hospital, my old man patched him in the club first thing, saying anyone who survived that ordeal deserved it. Now he's the sergeant at arms for the club and works here with me as the bouncer. He don't rile much, and fights don't happen often, but when they do, he takes care of it."

I shuddered a bit. I'd been through several rotations in the local hospital emergency room, and had seen some serious trauma done to the human body. Just the idea of what Mute had been through was terrifying, and I know would be enough to give anyone a sour outlook on life. I still stayed away from him as much as possible, and only went near him to refill his coffee cup. Knowing a bit of his story helped, but he was still one big, scary biker. Whenever I chanced a glance at him, his frown deepened.

The rest of the night was loud. Some baseball game was playing silently on the big screen, and the jukebox was blasting out country songs. Laughter and loud conversation competed with the machine's volume. Everyone was there to have a good time, to enjoy life and be a part of a bigger fellowship. I found myself relaxing even though I was running around like crazy, pouring beer into giant glasses and shots into small ones, popping bottle tops and collecting empties. I knew I would be tired later, but I still felt good, despite the minor run-in with Mute. I also met more of the club's old ladies. Molly was a loud, vivacious curly-haired blonde who literally strutted in her Silver brand jeans and Property of Cutter cut. Her ass twitched with every step of her stilettos. Tambre was older like Betsey, dark-haired and heavyset, with a generous bottom and top. She belonged to Taz, who was the club VP. These women were loud and fun, right at home in the bar. Their laughter rang out as they sat at the far left end of the bar, an area that was all but reserved for them. They were almost like celebrities, from the way most of the club patrons either knew them, or knew of them and admired them from afar.

The other women hanging around were cheap imitations of the real thing. They seemed to be in competition with each other to catch the attention of the male patrons by showing as much skin as possible. Supershort skirts, spiky heels or boots, tight tanks cut low—it was hard to tell one from the other. Big hair and heavy makeup rounded out what I was calling the "biker skank" look. The old ladies didn't need to work that hard at getting attention. They had a confidence about them; they knew who they were and where they belonged, and were secure in it. That made them and belonging to the club very attractive. This was the kind of family I'd always wanted to be a part of, and even if I wasn't part of it, at least I could watch and admire it from afar.

At the end of the night, Betsey cleared the tip jar and I had fifty-six dollars cash in my pocket. I could make fifty-six dollars last a long time at the grocery store or in the gas tank. As she handed me my portion, I couldn't help but smile in delight. This was the difference I needed in my life, especially today. I was sure tips were better on weekends, but if I could make just this little bit more every week, I would be able to survive and maybe even get Fred fixed soon.

"You ain't gonna quit, are you? You did real good, and I really need you here. Them club bitches just wanna hook up most nights, and I need someone reliable who's gonna show up and do the job," Betsey asked, her green eyes pleading.

"Mute didn't seem too happy with me here. Is he going to fire me?" I was a little surprised at Betsey approaching me that quickly, but I'd learned already she was a no-nonsense person. What was on her mind came out of her mouth.

"Oh, honey, you don't gotta worry 'bout Mute. He don't do no hiring an' firing here. His bark really is worse than his bite. Well, not for them folks who come in here to start trouble. He stops fights before they begin, so this place is safer than walking through town at night, and you know how empty them streets is."

I smiled with genuine affection for the older woman. I'd thought a few times about finishing out the night and not coming back, but being handed a much-needed wad of cash was a great incentive to continue working there. I could get used to Mute, even if he was scary.

"I need the job, so no, I'm not quitting. This works out perfectly with my schedule, at least for now."

I enjoyed the work. It was hard and kept me running in my sneakers all night, but aside from a little flirting from Stud, no one said much to me. I could work here and still be invisible, but also be around the bright light of the club women's circle. Just a little of that reflection felt wonderful, and I appreciated just being on the edge of that circle.

"Welcome to the family, darlin'!" she said with some relief.

**

Mute observed the bar as he always did, drinking coffee, and looking for problems. He already could feel the new help was going to be one. All night he had watched her, slipping through the crowd, deftly avoiding eye contact, staying out of people's way. She seemed to want to melt into the background, and in some ways that made her the perfect employee. One who would do her job and get things done with no muss or fuss. She didn't dress to impress, wearing jeans and plain T-shirt, simple sneakers, hair up in one of those stretchy things. It was hard to tell if she wore makeup or not.

When he had first walked into the bar, he'd been angry. Brick had called for a church meeting at the Lair earlier, and all the ranking members and officers had to be present. The older man had shown his frustration, banging the gavel repeatedly to maintain order at the formal meeting.

There was bad business going on around town, rumors of drug running, even though the club had gotten out of that shit years ago. Brick and Betsey had worked hard to get the club out of the one-percenter limelight and into legit businesses without feeling the loss of income, but people had long memories when it came to the bad stuff. He'd spent the afternoon searching corners with a club prospect, hanging around, looking for leads. Nothing. It was hard enough to make himself understood, let alone get anyone to communicate with him, and the prospect was either too scared or too stupid to try.

When he'd arrived at the bar tonight, he'd slumped heavily into his spot at the bar and tapped at the new girl for his coffee. She looked at him like she was ready to run out the door. Real pretty eyes, but fuck this shit! His patience was at an end. He stood up and thumped the bar again, knowing his frustration was showing and he was taking it out on an innocent girl. Betsey was there in an instant, talking fast and light, pouring his coffee. The girl settled and went back to work, steadily if uneasily.

Too soft, thought Mute. *Pretty girl but too soft for the life. Probably not stick it out. Leave in a week.*

CHAPTER THREE

"Just another few months, Fred, and then you can die peacefully. I promise."

I pulled into the familiar parking lot and got out of the shuddering vehicle. I'd been working at the River's Edge for several weeks, and my life had settled into a comfortable routine. I was getting better and better at tending the bar and memorizing more of the few drink recipes that were occasionally requested. The tips were great, and enough for me to save up some money.

"That thing's a death trap, darlin'. Shoulda been put outta its misery a year ago."

I jumped at the loud, gravelly voice and saw Mackie shuffling across the narrow parking area.

Mackie was one of the bar's regulars, although he was not a part of the MC. I had met him the second night I'd worked at the bar. He always came in for a few hours in the evening, and sat in the same seat at the bar. He was an older man, somewhere in his midseventies, always wearing old jeans and flannel work shirts. A baseball cap typically covered what was left of his grizzled gray hair, and he kept a bristly gray beard to match. He also had only one arm, the right sleeve of his shirt tucked neatly into the jeans pocket. The first night I met Mackie, he asked for a beer on tap.

"Which one?" I asked.

Mix'em up!" he declared, grinning at me. "Name's Mackie. You're new, ain'tcha?"

"Yes, sir. Started last night."

"Darlin', I ain't been a sir in a coon's age. Jus' call me Mackie. You like workin' here?"

"So far. I haven't had any trouble, and everyone is really nice."

"Yep. Good place. Good people. Gets a little rowdy every now and then, but Betsey runs a tight ship, and Mute takes care of trouble."

I'd only seen Mute sit at the end of the bar, drink coffee, and glower at people, but I wasn't going to argue. I went to set up a tab, as it seemed that Mackie was there to stay awhile. Mute thumped the counter next to me, and I automatically went to refill his cup. I was confused when I found it already full. I'd tried to avoid looking directly at him, so as to not make him mad, but he thumped the counter again. I raised my eyes to his hesitantly. He wasn't mad or fierce this time, but there was a firmness to his face. He pointed to the tab area near the register and shook his head.

"N-n-no tab?" I stammered. "P-p-pay as he goes?"

He shook his head again.

"Um... I'm confused. Does he pay at all?"

He shook his head yet again.

"Um... okay."

*Betsey appeared at my side, coming from the back
storage rooms with several bottles in her arms. "Hey,
darlin'. No need to fret. We don't charge him here. Mackie's
a Vietnam War vet. Lost his arm over there saving a whole
platoon of soldiers when he got blown out of a tank. His tab
was paid a long time ago."*

*My eyes watered slightly. I may have been working for
a rough MC bar, but Mackie was right. Good place, good
people.*

"I'm surprised that heap passes inspection," the old man
grumbled.

I laughed and waited for him to catch up to me.

"It probably wouldn't, so I haven't had it inspected
in a while," I quipped back. "Fred's been with me a long
time, but hopefully I can let him retire gracefully in a few
months."

He grunted as he reached me, rolling his eyes. I hugged
him, and we walked in side by side.

Mackie sat at his favorite spot, and I went behind the bar.
He reached out his hand as if holding a mug and gazed at it
with a sad, confused look on his face. I laughed, filled a mug
from a random tap, and placed it carefully in his cupped
palm. His expression immediately changed to one of happy
satisfaction, and he slurped at the frothy head.

I laughed again and happened to glance over at Mute,
who was sitting at his usual spot. His gaze was intense, and
for a moment I felt fear buzz through me. Then he nodded

both in greeting and approval.

I was getting more and more relaxed around Mute. I could interpret most of his signals and the few expressions he used. I'd still never seen him laugh or even crack a smile, but it seemed he had subtle ways of making himself understood—or at least, he did to me. Almost like a private dialogue I could hear in my head. I even assigned a voice to him, deep, masculine, one that would growl out words but underneath had the power to roar.

Mute thumped the bar twice, and I heard it as two syllables.

"Co-ffee."

I refreshed his cup and he nodded at me once, his dark eyes on mine and his mouth in its normal frown.

"Thanks," I heard in my head.

"Don't mention it," I replied, as if we were having a conversation. He looked a bit surprised at my response, but I decided to let it go. I had to get along with him and stop being scared of him.

"I'm going to make a round of the floor, clear some empties, and do a drink check. Okay with you, Betsey?"

"Sounds good darlin'." Betsey was at the bar running one of the blenders, probably for the margarita concoction she was known for making. Bruiser was the other bartender/ biker on duty. I didn't know how he got his club name, but it had nothing to do with the cute little Chihuahua that Reece Witherspoon toted around in that *Legally Blonde* movie. He was not much taller than me, but very round. He wore a blue work shirt under his cut that strained at the buttons to hold him in. His thinning hair was pulled back in a short ponytail that wasn't much more than a single curl. He was pulling beers as fast as he could, trying to keep up with the crowd. He grunted a "Hey, Kat" greeting with a quick tobacco-stained grin, and then went back to work.

It was a Friday night, early enough that the football game was still on, but late enough that most of the bar patrons were tanked. Stud's band was on the stage playing loud country rock. He was the bassist and lead singer. A row of club skanks were in front of them, screaming and dancing hard, trying their best to entice the band members. I knew two of them, Nikki and Donna, and they were the biggest of the skanks, ready to go to the back rooms of the bar or do whatever they had to do to get invited to the Lair. I glanced at Stud as I skirted the dance floor to get to the tables on the back wall. Nikki was singing off-key at the top of her lungs, jumping up and down so hard on her heels I was expecting her to either fall over or her unrestrained breasts to pop out of her low-cut top. I rolled my eyes at him and he grinned through the lyrics and winked at me.

Of all the bikers, Stud was the one who remembered my name first and never failed to greet me when he came in the bar. I'd heard he lived up to his club name quite often. In the short time I'd been working at the bar, he had taken several different women either to the back room or to the Lair. I wasn't surprised that he had his pick on a nightly basis. He was romance-book-model hot! Light golden-blond hair and icy blue eyes made him appear like a Viking warrior. All he needed was the horned helmet to complete the look. He was tall with broad shoulders, and his muscles were strongly defined under his tight T-shirts and club cut, but he wasn't bulky. He was the polar opposite of what I'd imagined a biker was, in that he had a full-fledged college degree in law, and was the club's accountant and lawyer. He came from a rich background and still had a ton of money, but something about the MC lifestyle called to him. He fit in perfectly. Normally someone like him wouldn't give someone like me the time of day or even notice I was in the room, but he was friendly and made a point of talking to me whenever we were in the same place. Since he was never more than friendly, and had never invited me to the Lair, I felt easy around him.

While I was walking through the crowd, a fight broke out between two men, something about the game on the TV or a woman. Maybe both. I don't know what it was, but it got bad pretty quick. One drunk threw a sloppy punch at the other, and then got tackled by his buddy. Soon a couple more men joined in the brawl, and before I could get out of the way, I was trapped between the back wall and the fighters. This was so not the best place to be! Fists and blood were flying. Tables were shoved out of the way; glasses and bottles crashed to the floor, covering it with leftover beer and broken glass. I pressed myself against the wall, trying to become smaller, praying to become invisible. The other people around the brawling men cleared the dance floor quickly, and I could see Stud moving off stage with his bass, his gaze searching for me as I cowered against the back wall. My eyes darted around, looking for a place to hide or a gap in the crowd to escape through, but I couldn't move without getting near the fighters. A bottle came flying through the air and smashed against the wall just above my head, covering me in beer and bits of glass. I gave a short scream and covered my head, crouching lower and trying to watch for more flying objects at the same time.

Mute was up and making his way into the fight. His usually calm and expressionless face was twisted in fury, lips pulled back in a feral snarl, his eyes flashing fire. He pulled one of the fighters out by grabbing the back of his shirt and literally tossing him across the room, with very little effort. His corded arms flexed as he grabbed the next one, throwing him around like a sack of potatoes. He paused long enough to glance at me, and quirk his eyebrow up.

"You okay?"

I couldn't speak, and he probably couldn't hear me over the angry shouting. I gave him a thumbs-up even though my knees were shaking. He jerked his head toward the bar.

"Move that way and get to the bar."

I hugged the wall as I eased my way around the twisting mass of men. The few seconds it took Mute to check on me bought him a fist in the face. He staggered back briefly before coming back at his assailant with a hard roundhouse to his jaw. The man went down and stayed down, knocked out cold. Mute spent a few more minutes jerking the fighters apart and throwing them to the side, but most of them broke off quickly after seeing that single punch.

A lot of the bar patrons had simply left when the fight started. The man on the floor woke up after his buddies poured a leftover beer on his head. They helped him to his feet and staggered out to the parking lot.

Betsey came up behind me. "You okay, darlin'?"

"Yeah, I'm good," I answered, still buzzing from the adrenaline. I smelled like old beer now. I went to shake my head as best as I could over the trash can to get out any little glass bits, but I was sure there was something still left in there.

"Go see to Mute. His lip's all cut up. Joni and I will get this mess cleared up. After that, you can go home and check the rest of your head for glass. You still got some in there."

I nodded, still in a bit of shock.

"You gonna quit?"

I blinked at the unexpected question. "Um... no?"

She smiled. "That's my girl! Tougher than you look!"

I went over to where Mute was sitting back in his usual spot. Mackie was grinning and reliving the fight like a kid in a candy store.

"Goddamn! That was some punch! Betcha knocked out a tooth or two. That sumbitch won't be back for a while!"

Mute fingered his bloody lip where the "sumbitch" had landed his fist, and thumped the bar sharply.

"Co-ffee."

I brought him a fresh cup. I couldn't quite look up, but felt I needed to say something to him.

"Thank you" was all I could manage.

He grabbed my wrist as I was turning away. I gasped and froze in surprise. His grip was warm and strong. He pulled me closer across the bar, his dark eyes deep and unreadable.

He reached toward my face, and pulled out three small pieces of glass that were still caught in my hair. I swallowed at the contact, feeling an unfamiliar warmth bloom in my gut. I couldn't look away, and for a small eternity we just stared at each other. He broke it off when he reached for the steaming mug, draining half of it.

"Top it off?" I asked, my voice a little breathy. I was sure he could hear my heart pounding. He nodded, and I refilled his mug.

Out of the corner of my eye, I saw Donna approach. I wasn't sure of her status in the MC; from what Betsey told me, she wasn't an old lady, but she had a place in the club. Donna wore the same "uniform" the other club skanks favored. Long, blonde hair that was way overbleached to the point of having a light green tint, tons of crusty makeup, supershort jean skirt with a torn hem, and a cut-off tank one size too small, showing off ridiculously large breasts. If she was wearing a bra, there wasn't much padding, as her hardened nipples showed through easily. She could barely walk in the red spiked fuck-me pumps she had on her feet, but she managed to sidle up to Mute.

I wrapped some ice cubes in a towel and brought it over to Mute. Donna was rubbing herself against him and cooing. He sat there stoically, his face set in his normal frown.

"That was so hot!" she trilled. I gritted my teeth at her grating voice. For some reason I didn't want her anywhere near Mute. "So strong!" She ran her hands over his arms and back, and pressed her breasts into his arm. I was surprised at how badly I wanted to slap her away from him. This wasn't me at all, and worse, it wasn't like there was a reason for me to feel this way.

I offered the towel-wrapped ice to Mute. "Your hand and lip are bleeding," I whispered. He looked up into my eyes, and I was drawn into his dark gaze. I couldn't read his expression, but I felt there was something there for me to see. My heart pounded.

Donna's squeal broke the connection. "Oh, Mutie! You're hurt!"

Mute didn't move. He was still looking at me deeply, not reacting at all to the ridiculous way Donna said his name. He wrapped the dripping towel around his swollen knuckles, and brought it up to his lip.

Mackie was still chuckling and reliving the brief fight. "Set me up with one more myself, darlin'. Yessir, that was one helluva punch!"

Betsey was over in the corner where I'd been trapped, sweeping up the last of the glass and talking into the cell phone lodged between her shoulder and ear. Donna was cooing something into Mute's ear, and still rubbing her hands all over him. Other Dragon members were back at the pool table, their game having been barely slowed by the fight. A few other diehard patrons were scattered around, but for the most part the bar was empty.

"Damn, that girl just doesn't give up!" Betsey came up behind me, shaking her head as she put away the broom and dustpan. "She's been teasing Mute for weeks at the clubhouse, trying to get in his bed. I've told her over and over again, he's not a man to play with."

She saw the confused look on my face and sighed. "It's part of club life, darlin'. There are two kinds of women in the club, old ladies and club bunnies. I know that's being real blunt, but that's how it is. Them girls that hang around the club looking for a good time? Them's the bunnies. They hop from one man to another faster than shit from a goose. No one treats 'em bad or beats on 'em. My boys ain't that kinda men. They got the same choice everyone else does. Donna wants to be an old lady, but no one here will take her that way on account as she's been with so many of their brothers already."

Betsey kept cleaning up during her monologue of information. I'd figured out that Betsey was a talker. She hated silence, and all you had to do was stay quiet for a bit and she would fill the air with words.

"Being an old lady is like being married, only better. You know my man, Brick, is the club president. We've been together for near on forty years now. We've been through lots of rough and lots of good. We got kids and grandkids now. He gave me a ring years ago, but we never sealed the deal. I don't need that paper and a preacher to know he's mine and I'm his. I know beyond a shadow of a doubt he loves me and would die to protect me. I stay out of the club business for the most part, and do what he needs me to do to help him out. He gave me this bar to run for him and the club. I know he's had a few other tastes over the years, but I'm still the one he comes home to every night, and will be until we leave this earth."

She dumped the broken glass into the nearest trash can

set out just for bottles.

"Mute is a challenge to them bunnies. He doesn't party much, doesn't drink or take a woman very often. They all want of a piece of him like he's a big prize. Something about the strong, silent type, I reckon. I've seen two or three of them up at the Lair, crawling all over him, showing him their tits and such. He don't pay no attention to none of it most of the time, but once in a while, he'll take one back to his room. Never seen him take one a second time." Betsey made her trademark pssht sound. "Donna needs to wake up. Mute ain't never gonna be interested in her for more than a night, if he ever does in the first place."

"Um… okay," I stuttered, glancing over at Donna still pressed to Mute, running her fingers through his hair. He sat stoically, just sipping his coffee, the melting ice dripping on the counter from his wrapped hand. He seemed to be completely ignoring her, but he wasn't exactly pushing her away.

"You all right? You ain't thinkin' about quittin' now, are you?"

Betsey is really hung up on this quitting thing. "No, I'm not going to quit. I just keep thinking about this one thing."

"What's that, darlin'?"

Time to break the tension a bit. I grinned at her. "Mutie? Seriously?" I choked out, trying to stifle my laugh.

Betsey threw her head back and laughed, both in humor and relief. Mute glared at both of us. "I've been so afraid you'll get overwhelmed and leave. I should have known better. Not everyone is cut out for this life. Even working around it can be a challenge."

"I'm done for the evening too, ladies. See you tomorrow night!" Mackie declared, as if nothing had happened.

Betsey shooed him off with a smile. Stud appeared at the bar, his blue eyes full of worry.

"You okay, Kat? I tried to get to you, but I couldn't see where you'd gone."

I felt my face flush at his concern. "I'm okay. Nothing a hairbrush and shower won't take care of."

"I need to pack up. Are you okay to drive? I'll take you home when I'm done, unless you want to go to the Lair. It's probably closer, and we've got showers and stuff up there."

My mouth dropped open at the coveted invitation to visit the famed private compound that so many people tried to get into. He looked into my eyes, waiting for a response, and I could feel the others looking at me. I'd heard many times about Stud and his almost nightly array of partners. I'd even seen him charm the pants off a woman, literally! Usually an invite to the Lair with Stud meant an invite to his bed, but he didn't seem to be giving me the same act he did when he was out for a good time. I decided he was just being a concerned friend more than anything else. I was kind of relieved, as it would be too much pressure to try to live up to Stud's image. Any of the women who were hanging around him earlier would jump at the chance to go to the Lair, especially with him. I was sitting there with a golden opportunity I was too scared to take.

Mute's mug came crashing down on the bar hard enough that coffee dregs sloshed over the side. The noise broke my trance, and I looked over at him. Mute finally had had enough of Donna hanging on him, and had left his bar spot, walking out the door, leaving her standing in confusion.

Betsey just rolled her eyes. "Take my advice, girl. Find someone else. Mute ain't interested, and I doubt any of the other boys will make an old lady out of a woman who has been public property so long."

Donna pouted. "He's probably just tired from the fight. He'll take me to the Lair sometime soon."

"What about you, Kat?" Stud was still waiting. "You want to come to the Lair and clean up, or go home."

I flushed again and felt a little panic. I decided it was best to retreat and become invisible again.

"Umm... thanks for the invite up there, but I'd best go on home. I have stuff to do in the morning, and a study group tomorrow afternoon. I'll be okay getting there on my own."

His eyebrows came together. I got the feeling that not many women turned him down. Maybe I was wrong. "I'll at least follow you home."

I shook my head and laughed, trying again to break the sudden tension. "Don't bother. I'm cleaning up and going straight to bed. You need to get up to the Lair anyway, don't you? Your band is going to play up there for a bit, right?"

"Yeah, we are. Tell you what, hand me your phone," he demanded.

I gave him my ancient slider with its tiny screen. He gave me a look and rolled his eyes at the old phone as he programmed his number into it. A moment later, his fancy smartphone started singing an old Def Leppard song. "Pour Some Sugar on Me" was now my ringtone in Stud's phone.

"You have my number now. When you get in safely, you text me. If I don't hear from you in the next half hour, I'm coming down the hill. Got me?"

I bit my lower lip just to have something to do. No one had looked out for me in a long time, and being cared for left a warm feeling in my belly. That scared me. I didn't want to get used to it. When it happened, it was only a matter of time before it was ripped out from under me.

I plastered a smile on my face that I hoped looked relaxed and genuine. "I got you. Thanks, Stud. This means a lot to me."

He still wasn't happy, but he let me walk out the door to my car by myself. I went to where my car was parked. I could hear the burble of the river just beyond the fenced area of the lot. It startled me to see Mute sitting on his massive black bike, parked just on the other side of my car. The yellow glow of the outside safety light lit up his face, making him look predatory. A very handsome predator. That warmth in my belly clenched both in fear and fascination. He raised a cigarette to his lips and took a short drag. He looked behind me, and then back at me with his eyebrow raised in question.

"You going to the Lair with Stud?"

I shook my head and opened my car door.

"No, I'm not going to the Lair tonight. I have too much to do tomorrow, and I'd rather go home."

He was still for a moment, then he nodded and dropped

the half-smoked cigarette and crushed it out with his booted foot.

"Good," I heard in my head.

I bit at my bottom lip again and dropped my eyes. He snapped his fingers to get my attention and then held his finger and thumb up to his mouth and ear as if using a phone. He reached his other hand with large palm open, out to me.

"Gimme your phone."

For the second time that night, a hot biker programmed his number into my phone while frowning at its age. A moment later his phone beeped with a text to put my number in his phone. No fancy ringtone for me there.

"Text me when you get home." His gestures and look echoed Stud almost perfectly.

"I will," I said, taking back my phone. "Stud wants me to text him too. I'll be fine." His expression said nothing else.

I know he was just doing his job, but still he had come to my rescue and had gotten hurt because of it. I felt I had to say something. "Thank you again, Mute, for helping me tonight. You have no idea how much that means to me."

His eyes glittered as they bored into mine. That belly clench bloomed with sudden heat.

I left, not trusting myself to say anything more. The night had been overwhelming, between the fight in the bar and the attention I received from not one but two of the hottest club members. I needed to get invisible, and fast.

***

Mute sat on his bike and watched the taillights of Kat's

rust bucket Taurus disappear. He'd overheard her refer to her car as Fred once or twice. Fuck! She actually named that firetrap! Wouldn't be long before Fred needed to be renamed Dead Fred, by the sound of the engine. He spat on the ground, trying to get the bitter cigarette taste out of his mouth. He didn't smoke often, mostly because Betsey didn't want it in the bar, but also because he didn't want anything to control him. Once in a while, though, after a really bad night, the craving got to him.

Craving. Fuck! Mute clenched his fists over and over, feeling the bruised skin tighten over his knuckles. The panic he'd felt when he'd seen Kat against the wall, terrified and covered in glass, still sat in his gut. The need to protect her was heavy, and he didn't know where it was coming from.

Just my job. I woulda done the same for Betsey or any of the other girls.

But if it had been Betsey, she would have come out swinging herself and probably kicked some ass before he even got off his barstool. He fingered the scabbing split in his lip, unsure that he would have shown so much concern for any of the other girls, getting distracted enough to be sucker punched.

Fuck this! he thought furiously. Kat was too damn soft, not made for the life. She just needed to get the hell gone.

He cranked up his bike; its sleek power rumbled under him. He saw Stud come out of the bar, his arm around a random band groupie who had been dancing with several others around the front of the stage all night. He lifted her chin with his hand and kissed her hard. Looked like some serious tongue action was going on. Stud climbed on his bike and the groupie climbed on behind him. He grinned at her over his shoulder, and took off toward the entrance to the Lair.

Mute watched him go. Like smoking, getting laid by random women wasn't something he did often. Most women at the bar took one look at his hard face and backed off. The regular pussy at the club was always available. Donna would fuck him in a heartbeat, but he knew she had thoughts of being his old lady, and that was something that wasn't going to happen. He sat on the purring bike, the craving for another cigarette growing.

Fuck! Maybe I do just need to get laid, he thought, looking at the security gate that led to the Lair. Donna was still around, and had made it clear she was available. Mute grimaced. *Not tonight. Don't need that shit. Too much headache to deal with later.* He spat on the ground again, turned his bike, and drove away from the bar in a spray of gravel, heading home.

CHAPTER FOUR

The bar was packed the next night. Stud's band was playing somewhere else, and a bigger touring band was playing here. It felt like everyone in Bryson City had come out to see them. Either that, or word had gotten around about the fight and people wanted a front-row seat if the show was going to be repeated. The area reserved for dancing was packed with gyrating bodies, mostly female. Their squeals filled the air, almost overtaking the band.

It was busy enough even in the fall months that Betsey had hired another waitress. I was serving on the floor and running around like crazy trying to keep up with drink orders, and bussing tables. Bruiser was back at the bar pouring and mixing alongside Betsey. Mute was at his usual spot, drinking his coffee and glowering at anyone who got too close to him. A few of the other Dragons were there as well, drinking, enjoying the music, and flirting with anyone in a short skirt.

I was clearing a table full of glasses and empty bottles

when for some reason, I looked up and saw Mute staring at me. No, not staring, glaring in deep anger. My heart dropped to the pit of my stomach as my brain started running through all the ways I could have pissed him off. Shit! Did I remember to text him last night along with Stud?

Then I heard a sardonic voice right behind me. "Got some new talent in the pool, I see."

I jumped a little and turned to see two club members I had not met yet. The one who had spoken had the name Joker sewn on his cut, and the other had Box.

"Just a hint, baby, you'll get better tips if you work your stuff in shorts and heels. That ass is fine in them jeans, but the sneakers gotta go. What's your name?"

"I'm... um... Katrina," I stuttered. Joker was like Stud in that he had blond hair and blue eyes, but that's where the similarities ended. His hair was cut in a Mohawk and the sides of his shaved head were tattooed with a row of dancing harlequin skulls. He had a ring piercing in his eyebrow and lip.

"Well, Um Katrina, how's about getting me and my friend here a beer? Something on tap. And give it a good *head*."

He drew out the word head and reached between his legs to grab himself. I swallowed, not trusting myself to speak. I just turned and walked quickly to the bar to get their beers. Bruiser was frowning as he filled the heavy glass mugs.

"Joker's harmless, sweetheart, but there's bad blood between him and Mute. Brother or not, he ain't happy that bastard's here. Watch yourself," he intoned as he finished pulling the beer and loaded my tray.

I brought the tall foaming glasses to them at the table they had taken over, and set them down on paper coasters in front of them.

"Kat, Kat, Kat," Joker chanted. "Itty bitty pretty kitty Kat."

I moved to leave, but he grabbed my arm, pulling me onto his lap. I squeaked as I lost my balance, trying not to drop the serving tray or fall on the floor.

"What's your hurry, pussy Kat? Not much of a cat, are you? More like a mouse. Quiet little mousie." His singsong tone was more menacing than playful.

My heart was racing with the need to escape. "Please let me up, I have work to do."

He gave me a fake crestfallen look and whined, "Aw, but we're having such a good time, right, Box? I just wanna play with the pussy Kat for a minute. 'S been a while since I petted one."

He held me down on his lap and I could feel him getting hard underneath my bottom. He started grinding against me, and shoved his nose in my neck, sniffing deeply.

"Mmmm... yeah! Fresh new talent! You goin' to the Lair after work tonight, baby? I can pet that pussy all night. Make it *purr*." He rolled the r in purr. I felt the panic rise in my throat. Part of being invisible meant I didn't have to deal with harassment very often and usually it came in the form of catcalls and a few whistled suggestions. I'd never really been scared of it as I was now. The feeling of being physically restrained and forced to feel Joker's growing erection was terrifying. I struggled a bit on Joker's lap and tried to sound firm. "No, I'm not going to the Lair. I have work to do, so please let me up."

I sounded more like I was begging.

Joker laughed and held on tighter, running one arm around my hips to hold me down, and the other over my bottom.

"Oh, pussy Kat, pussy Kat! The things I'm going to do to this ass!"

A hand came down on the table with a bang loud enough to make me think it split the wood. I ceased my struggles and looked up into the absolutely furious eyes of Mute. I knew then what it felt like to be that mouse caught between two predatory cats.

Joker laughed again.

"Well, hello to you too, Mute. Long time no see!" He relaxed his hold on me, and I tried to stand, only to have him tighten his arms around me again. I swear Mute all but growled.

"Whatsa matter, Mute? Kat got your tongue? How does she taste?" He went into peals of laughter at his own crude joke, and threw his arms wide open. I leapt up and out of the way. Mute reached for my arm and pulled me behind him.

"Is she yours, Mute? You done claimed a woman?" Joker gasped between laughs. "Thought you were done with that shit!"

Betsey hollered across the barroom. She was laughing and smiling, but it didn't reach her eyes. Her voice rang out in authority. "Joker, you quit messing with my help!

Kat's a good girl! You chase her off, I'm gonna put your ass in an apron an' have you start sweeping up an' serving! Go up to the Lair and find a woman there, ya horny bastard!"

"Betsey, my one true love!" Joker hollered back. "When are you gonna dump that useless old man of yours and run away with me?" He stood up, one arm flung out to the side and the other placed across his chest, palm flat over his heart. He showed a leg and executed a courtly bow.

Just like that the tension was broken. Joker became his namesake. Loud, cracking jokes on everything and anyone. The life of the party. His friend Box sat as his wingman for the rest of the night, and both Donna and Nikki glued themselves to them. Donna sat firmly on Joker's lap, while Nikki rubbed against Box. Their squeals grated against my ears every time they called for another round.

"No hard feelin's, right, Pussy Kat? I was just jokin' with you," Joker said to me while he was squeezing Donna's ample ass.

I placed the latest round on the table and picked up the empties.

"Sure, no problem," I muttered, and tried to smile at him. My belly was still quivering with fight or flight instinct, leaning more toward flight.

He grabbed my wrist. His eyes hit mine. His voice was light, but his eyes were serious. "You really with Mute?"

Donna huffed in protest. "She ain't with anyone, baby. She's just here to help Betsey until she gets outta nursing school," she slurred. She was completely drunk, stroking the shaved part of his head and licking his neck.

"Is that right? Well then, Pussy Kat, anytime you feel like playing doctor, you can call me."

He let me go. Donna huffed again at his words, and then burst into drunken giggles when he stood up and hefted her over his shoulder.

"See y'all later!" he yelled out to the bar. "I gotta go give a full examination to this woman! Box, where's my anal probe!"

He and Box left, I guessed to go to the Lair. I was able to breathe easier without him in the building.

Betsey was wiping the bar when I finally got a chance to sit for a minute. The other old ladies were there too.

"Don't pay no mind to Joker, darlin'. He's a club member, but currently a nomad, and wanders in from time to time. He ain't never here too long so we don't hafta deal with him much. He just likes to party and make trouble, but he's all mouth. Let me know if he gets to be too much."

Molly chimed in with more concern. "I don't know, Betsey. He may not be as harmless as you think. He's always been shifty. His daddy was one of the defectors way back when. Then there was the thing with Mute."

Betsey stopped wiping the bar and looked Molly in the eye. Her direct gaze was not one I'd ever want on me.

"That was a long time ago, and that hatchet was buried. We've moved on. Mute's moved on. The club moved on. You need to let it rest."

Molly pursed her lips but didn't say anything. She followed my habits, dropped her eyes, and became invisible, or as invisible as a biker's old lady could get.

Two thumps on the counter distracted me. Mute added a third one.

"Co-ffee, now."

I hurried to fill his cup. His face was dark and brooding, still angry at Joker. Clearly he was not as forgiving of Joker's antics as Betsey was. His hand clutched at the white mug so hard, I thought it might break. I could still see some bruising there, and around his lip where the brawler had sucker punched him. He'd rescued me two times now, from last night's fight and from being accosted by Joker. I didn't know where this was going, but I liked it. I liked feeling that someone had my back, at least here at the bar. All my life, it was just me. My last set of foster parents weren't bad people, but I was never really part of their family. I was always the extra, identified as "my foster kid" rather than "my daughter." More and more each day, I was getting the sense of belonging somewhere, of having people who cared enough to help and defend me, of having a family.

Mute managed to shatter that feeling in a matter of minutes.

"Thanks again, Mute," I said quietly. "Anything else I can get for you?"

Mute looked in my eyes and scowled furiously. He was mad at me! Not what I expected. He pulled out his phone and rapidly texted something. My phone beeped, and I slid open the top to see what he'd sent.

Mute: Quit making trouble. Stay away from Joker and Stud. I'm getting tired of saving your ass for stupid shit.

He slammed his phone down and picked up his white coffee mug, sucking back more of the black brew.

I could feel my throat closing up. I didn't trust myself to speak. I didn't start the fight last night, I just got caught in it. I didn't flirt or seek out Stud, he came to me. I didn't throw myself in Joker's lap, he pulled me there and wouldn't let me go. How was any of this my fault?

Mute sat there at the end of the bar in his usual place, drinking his coffee, judging me as unworthy. For some reason, the unfairness was more than I could handle and I felt anger rush through me. Normally, I would have nodded, or murmured something and turned away. Instead, I slid my phone closed and slipped it into my back pocket. I looked back at him as he rested both tattooed arms on the bar, the mug held between his hands.

"Thanks again for your help, but you're an asshole."

He blinked in surprise. I guess he didn't expect the mouse to fight back.

I finished out the night, ignoring him as best I could, only filling his mug when he thumped the bar, and not speaking or making eye contact. I drove home in my protesting car and went straight to bed. I could hear Sheila and Chip in the next room, their sounds loud enough to cover up any noise my tears made.

* * *

Fuck, Fuck, Fuck!

Mute stepped outside the bar, ripping open his cigarette pack and nearly dumping the little white sticks on the ground in his fury. He clamped one between his lips, lit it, and sucked deep.

Fucking Joker! As a part of the club, Joker was a brother, and Mute took the code seriously, but he still loathed the man, his jokes, his presence, and everything else about him. It was a real struggle to have to take the back of someone he hated. Betsey liked him and his antics well enough to want to keep the peace, but Mute would rather he go away. Far, far away.

Goddamn! Shit! He threw the barely touched cigarette down, stomping on it angrily. He could've tolerated the man's loud presence in the bar, as he only ever stayed for a few days in one place, but when he put his hands on Kat, Mute saw red. Her fear had been palpable, and his only thought was getting her off that fucker's lap. He was probably balls deep in Donna by now, up at the Lair. But Kat? Hell no! Asshole needed to *bleed* for touching her!

Mackie strolled out of the bar. "I'm surprised Brick puts up with that sumbitch!" he declared. His one arm twitched uncontrollably for a moment, and he peered up at Mute. "You all right, boy? That rat bastard will be gone again come tomorrow. He just likes to stir up trouble. Kat didn't get hurt, and she's stronger than you think. She can handle him."

Fucking Kat! Mute looked down at the shredded cigarette. He was feeling guilty about his texted words to her. The fight in the bar wasn't her fault. She was just there at the wrong place and time. He also knew she didn't start anything with Joker. Hell, she went out of her way to *not* attract attention. Dressing plainly, not a lot of makeup, and sneakers, for Christ's sake! Problem was, she still had his attention. Every shift she worked, he watched her. He saw her smile, her kindness to Mackie, her laughter with Betsey, and the care she showed for the people around her. He wished she would shine some of that goodness his way, but whenever she found him looking at her, she would shutter that glow, drop her eyes, and avoid him as much as she could. He knew he did it to himself, pushing her away with his rough words and manners. He shouldn't have lashed out at her earlier, but it was for the best. Maybe she'd get the hint and move on. Mackie was wrong. She was too sweet and fragile for this life, and needed protection, even from him. Especially from him.

Mute nodded an "I'm fine" to Mackie, and flicked a hand towards his bike. The old man chortled. It was a treat for him to ride on the back of it. With one arm, it was awkward to hold on, but Mute figured the war vet deserved whatever happiness he could get. He put his thoughts about Kat down for the night and guided the bike slow and steady as he took Mackie home.

CHAPTER FIVE

October brought a burst of color in the North Carolina mountains. The summer green of the trees turned to rusty reds, yellows, golds, and browns. The official tourist season was over, but there were still plenty of people visiting the area to see the colors, ride the Great Smoky Railroad, and camp in the cooler fall weather. The beauty of the mountains was all around me, and I loved seeing it every day.

The bar was closing earlier than in the summer months. Betsey summed it up by saying most people don't want to stay out late when it gets cold at night, and any of the boys hanging around the bar can go hang at the Lair. This worked out well for her, as she was spending more time with her grandkids after school and on weekends. I'd heard that Blue and Jonelle were having problems again, and he had to call Betsey more often for help. This also worked well for me, in that I was deep into the last semester of classes before beginning the intern work at the hospital. I had to cover more hours at the bar to give Betsey time for Cody and Michelle, but it still worked out as I could study when I wasn't too busy at the bar. Mute came in nightly, but during the daytime hours, it was usually just the club ladies.

"Pretty dead, even for a Monday," Molly said, glancing around the nearly empty bar. Stud was at one corner table with a bunch of papers spread out. He was wearing reading glasses, which made him look hotter, even though the scholarly look was in contrast to his biker cut. My books were open on the end of the bar that Mute usually occupied. He wouldn't be in for a while, so I didn't see a need to move them yet. Taz and Cutter were in the back office with Brick. Tambre was at the bar with Molly, and Betsey was sitting with them instead of behind the bar with me. It was like the school library where everyone was working on something, including the old ladies.

"Cutter's got the hogs ready to go. Think five should be enough? We only got five big smokers, so if we need more meat, we either have to get another smoker or start earlier and get more done ahead of time." Tambre had her glasses on as well, and was perusing a list written on a yellow legal pad.

"Five was plenty last year, and we had more than enough food from the potluck pickin's," Betsey stated, tapping out a text on her phone. How she could do anything with those talons of hers, I'd never know.

"I'm more concerned about the candy. We came real close to running out last year. I want to get an extra fifty pounds to be sure."

"Fifty?" Molly shouted. "You think we'll need that much?"

Betsey stopped tapping. "Supposed to have more kids and more families coming in. More reservations for bigger tents, and the camping cabins are already full, even the big ones. I reckon we may get another two hundred before it's over with."

The ladies were going over the plans for one of the club's biggest events. Every year, the club hosted a community Halloween festival and barbecue at their biggest campground, about fifteen miles outside Bryson City. It was one giant party and fundraiser for a local charity. There were craft vendors that set up to sell handmade soaps, candles, knitted items, mountain art, and anything else you might find at a county fair. There weren't any fair rides, as there was not enough room to set up that much stuff, but there were lots of games for kids and adults set up by local churches.

Betsey's domain was the bar to be set up in the campground community house at the pavilion. The club donated and cooked the barbecue, and local people brought side dishes and desserts. Everyone was asked to make a donation to the box at the giant covered picnic area where the food would be set up. The money was given to the local children's home. The highlight of the afternoon was the Dragon's Tail Run hosted by the club members. Anyone twelve years old and up with parental permission could get on the back of a member's bike and be invited to "run the tail." Bikes would be roaring and running most of the day with screaming excited children on the backs. Brick was very careful about who he had doing the runs, as the Tail of the Dragon was not a road to take lightly. Over three hundred twisting curves in an eleven-mile stretch of road between North Carolina and Tennessee, the Tail was a motorcyclist's wet dream. The Dragon Runners got their name from the famous road, and owned several biker and campground resorts at both ends.

A map of the Tail was on the bar next to the planning list. My eyes widened a bit at the detailed curves and sharp switchbacks. Betsey tapped the map and filled me in on some club history and legend.

"Brick's grandpa, Old Jesse, was the one who gave him the idea, and his daddy, Jesse Jr., started the club after World War II. Old Jesse was a 'shine runner way back during them prohibition years and used to run the Tail in his classic Pontiac GTO, carrying moonshine across the state line. That was the best way to get away from the revenuers back then. Legend is he could make a night run on the Tail in less than twenty minutes. That would be some ride!"

Molly chimed in, "Lord, you know it! Taz's best time is twenty-two minutes on the short run. Takes over an hour and a half on the full run."

Tambre turned to me and explained. "The short run starts at the campground base and runs just above Deal's Gap into Tennessee." She pointed to a deep curve on the map just after the border. "They turn around here where Parson's Branch road is, and come back. This is the run they do for the kids. Adults who want to do the fun run have to wait, as there is only one for Halloween and it's long. We have a backup truck follow in case of any trouble."

"Brick's daddy, Jesse Jr., still ran 'shine like Old Jesse, but started running other stuff as well, for other people." Betsey added with a serious look on her face. She titched her teeth.

"Not a good time," Tambre noted. "The club was running drugs and guns through the Tail. Making a lot of money, but all the risk was on the brothers, not the ones doing the deals. More than one Dragon Runner left his blood on the Tail. Cutter's dad was one of them."

Betsey kept going. I was getting a bit dizzy from trying to take in all the information.

"Brick got tired of seeing his brothers risking their lives bein' not much more than errand boys. He started investing in other businesses like the resort campgrounds, the garage, this bar, and other ones around the area. He started recruiting members that wanted something cleaner for their families, but would still allow them to make the kind of money they were used to. People who wanted to live clean and ride free.

"It took time, and when Brick made the break, it got ugly. There was blood spilled on both sides, but we got the club out, and got it clean. Not everyone wanted the Dragon Runners to go legit, and there are still some people out there who resent us for gettin' out of that business. Said we'd gone soft, but I'll tell you now, my Brick ain't never been soft. I say it takes a hard man to make hard decisions, and even harder to stick by 'em. It's still not completely over, but we've moved up and on. We're in high cotton now, and Brick and I aim to keep it that way."

Mute came in the door at that moment, heralded by a

chorus of "Hey, Mute." I looked up and then away. We were on a truce. The last personal words between us were him telling me to quit causing trouble and me calling him an asshole. For the last few weeks, our communications were mostly in my head, with an occasional text. He'd ask for coffee, tell me to run out a tab, or take a beer and bottle inventory. Once or twice he texted me to check on Mackie, as the older man's shaking hand was getting worse.

Mute: Mackie's on some new pill. Don't look like it's helping much. Find out what it is and what it does.

He had texted yesterday afternoon while I was in class. I wanted to humph at his rudeness, but I was very fond of the Army vet and was concerned about his health as well. I'd done some research on the medication, and now went over to move my books, pour Mute his ever-present coffee, and tell him what I'd found out.

"I looked up Mackie's medication, and it's pretty powerful stuff," I said, setting his white mug down with a small thump. The women were back at their plans, all three heads leaning together, talking and taking notes.

I explained the medicine further, wiping the clean bar with a rag and trying not to look at Mute directly.

"In a nutshell, it helps to regulate the flow of dopamine in the brain so he can control his movements better. It's pretty risky in that there could be periods of time when it works and when it doesn't. I think that depends on the dosage, which has to be carefully regulated. There are also a lot of side effects, like nausea, confusion, dizziness, dry mouth, abdominal pain. It's probably not a good idea for him to be drinking at all with this stuff in his system."

I risked a glance up.

Mute rubbed his hand across his face. He looked tired, which was rare for him. He ignored his full cup and pulled out his phone, tapping the screen rapidly. My phone beeped and I pulled it out.

Mute: He's in rough shape rite now. The last stuff they had him on tore him up bad. He couldn't shit for a week and was seeing bugs on the walls. This stuff had him fighting war demons in his head again. He's finally asleep and should stay that way.

Mute's concern for the old man touched me, and I melted a little toward him. Behind his badass biker persona, I could see glimpses of a man who was more protector and warrior than tough and untouchable.

"Keep me in the loop and let me know if he needs help," I said out loud.

Stud came up to Mute, still wearing his glasses perched on the end of his nose and holding a handful of papers. My heart jumped a little when he threw his devastating smile at me. Mute just frowned deeper.

"Hey, Kat. Hitting the books hard, I see."

I flushed a bit. "Exams coming up. I have to qualify before I can go on the nursing floor."

"I'm sure you'll make it. Mute, I need to go over some things with you. Something's off with the books." Stud motioned for Mute to join him at his table.

I wiped down the bar, and headed back to where the ladies were making their plans and cackling. Now it was about Halloween costumes.

"Hey, Kat, what are you going to be?" Molly asked. "Gypsy, belly dancer, witch?"

"I hadn't really thought about it. I doubt I'll dress up." I turned to Betsey. "Do I have to?"

Betsey laughed. "Not really, but if you look at the twinkle in Molly's eye, she's 'bout to take you on as a project."

I wasn't so sure I wanted Molly to take me on as a project. She dressed nicely for the most part, but was definitely into the biker babe look. Her hair was always teased out, and she wore a lot of leather. Her makeup was tasteful, but a bit on the heavy side. More than I ever wore at one time.

Molly did look excited at the idea of dressing me up. She clapped her hands together. "Oh, this will be great! I know exactly what you'll be. Just leave it to me! Betsey, make sure she's off Friday night so I have enough time to get her sorted."

Betsey laughed and blew out a *pssht* as her phone rang. "Don't you go turning her into some sort of vampire slut! We already got enough of those hanging around, so keep it covered!"

Molly sat up, feigning offense. "I'll have you know, it *is* possible to be sexy without being slutty! It's all attitude. Showing as much skin as you can is slutty. I got something else in mind." She turned to me, noting my concerned look. "I promise you'll like it. Just trust me darlin'. Them boys won't know what hit them!"

This did not make my worried mind easy, but my thoughts were interrupted by Betsey's sudden yell.

"Are you shittin' me?" Her voice was loud and tight with anger. "When? How long? Okay. Okay, Perry, thanks. I'm on my way."

She jabbed the screen with her finger and all but threw the phone across the bar. I noticed that when she was angry or emotional the country in her came out more in her accent, and her profanity level rose significantly.

"That useless, life-sucking bitch!" she yelled at the top of her lungs. She jerked her purse from behind the bar and grabbed her jacket. "That was Perry down at the Sheetz gas station near River Street. Jonelle done left the kids alone again. Shells got off the bus and found Cody playing in the backyard by hisself. They're locked out of the house. Ain't got no spare key, and Jonelle ain't around. No neighbors home neither. Shells knows to go see Perry if'n there's a problem and she cain't call her daddy. Imma gonna kill that stupid bitch!"

She jerked on her leather jacket. "Kat, I need a big favor. Brick has a church meeting tonight at the Lair. Stuff having to do with the club and some happenings around town. I need you to run the bar up there for me. It's gonna go long, so you might be spending the night. Blue's on a run up to Tennessee for the sheriff, and will come directly home to his kids. He ain't gonna be at the Lair at all, so you can take his room tonight if you need it."

I blinked. "What about here?"

"Close it in a half hour and put a sign on the door saying family emergency. Not enough people right now to stay open anyway. I'll pay you time and a half for tonight. Molly,

Tambre, help her out if you can."

She turned to the back corner and yelled. "Mute! Stud! I gotta get to my grandkids! Kat's gonna cover for me tonight! Keep an eye on her and keep her safe. Use Blue's room if she needs it!"

Tambre spoke. "Get going, Betsey. Call me if you need me."

Mute came up, his expression thunderous, blocking Betsey and gesturing wildly. Betsey held a hand up in front of his face, and yelled at him in her own fury.

"I ain't got time to deal with you, Mute. My grandkids are someplace they don't need to be. Get over yourself and take care of business! I gotta go!"

With that she left, her fingers dialing her phone with sharp jabs. Mute turned his burning gaze on me.

"What the fuck have you done now?!" I heard in my head.

I knew I hadn't done anything to warrant his fury, and was torn between putting my own hand up angrily in his face or trying to shrink into the floor. I was leaning more toward the floor thing.

"Damn that skanky bitch!" Molly declared. She looked at me. "I'm on duty tonight at the station, but I'll stay as long as I can. Tambre, you're watching your grandkids tonight, right? Can you stay for a bit at the Lair after? At least until church is done? Probably not. You may have to solo for a bit tonight, Kat, and it's bound to be a doozy. Betsey wasn't kidding about you staying the night up there as the meeting's gonna go real long and the drinking after will keep on until tomorrow morning. Best to stay safe instead of crashing your car because you're too tired to see the road. If you don't feel right, Mute and Stud will be there after the church meeting and you can always hide in Blue's old room. No one will bother you there."

Stud had finished getting the papers in order, stacked, and back in a rolling briefcase. I would have laughed at the sight of a leather-clad biker in reading glasses with a fancy office briefcase if I wasn't so stunned at having to go to the Lair in a few hours.

"She can stay in my room. It's farther away from the main room, and has a double lock," he stated calmly, and winked at me.

My eyes widened a bit. The idea that I would need a double lock was just a bit intimidating. "I won't stay all night. If I'm too tired, I'll find a ride and just go home at some point when I'm not needed."

Stud took the glasses off his face and looked at me, ignoring the hostile vibes coming from Mute. "Betsey's right in that it's gonna go long tonight. Let's play it by ear. I've got an extra toothbrush, and you can use one of my tees to sleep in if you want it. If you really want to go home later, I'll take you."

Mute practically roared in my head, stomping around the bar, shaking his hands and head. It was abundantly clear he wanted me nowhere near the Lair. Why, I didn't know, but now was not the time to argue.

Molly clapped her hands together again. "Right. Let's get the bar sorted and closed. We can clean up tomorrow and resume the barbecue planning then."

* * *

Mute felt like the scowl on his face had become permanent. He was more frustrated than angry, but he knew that lately he looked perpetually furious at the world. *It's not Kat's fault this is happening,* he told himself. *Betsey's gotta take care of her grandkids since that shit-for-brains mom of theirs can't get her head outta her ass!*

Still, the thought of Kat at the Lair filled him with a simmering rage. Just because Betsey didn't allow drugs at the clubhouse didn't mean the members drank tea, ate little cookies, and talked about the weather or stock market! It was still a rough place, too rough for someone like Kat. The men got loud, drunk, and horny. The women did the same. A lot of drinking and plenty of random sex happened. It wasn't unusual to see a member getting a blow job from a club woman in public—most of the time that shit went to a back room or a cabin—but tonight the Lair would be full with visiting chapter members for a full church meeting with Brick, and the bunnies would be busy all night keeping everyone happy. Stud was concerned about the accounts. Meth dealers had been spotted in Bryson City, and there were rumors about the drug pipeline starting up again. Too much shit was going down. Kat was going to be in the middle of one of the rowdiest party nights the club would have this year, and there was nothing he could do about it.

Goddamn! he silently yelled as he left the bar to head to the Lair. The look in her eyes earlier when she was explaining Mackie's medicines showed how much she cared about the old man. He'd felt an urge to reach across the bar, pull her to him, and kiss her. All that sweet in her had to taste good, and he wanted some of it. Wanted it bad, but it wasn't for him.

Mute jammed a hand over his face again. He was tired from his shift at the bar last night, helping Mackie through his nightmares during the day, and fighting his feelings for Kat. He was facing another long night with club business and watching Kat's back among the strangers that would be there tonight. He had to stay strong and sure, but damned if something wouldn't break soon.

CHAPTER SIX

The Lair was not what I expected. It was more like one of the campground resorts the club owned. At the end of the steep drive was what could only be described as a log cabin lodge in a cleared flat area on the top of the hill. A lit gravel pathway was off to one side, blending into the woods and circling back. A bunch of one-room camping cabins were visible from the path, each with a different name burned into the door. The lodge was two stories high, had a wraparound porch complete with several swings on the lower half, and a full deck on the upper. Behind the lodge was a huge deck surrounding a large in-ground pool now covered for the winter. Several storage buildings were off to the other side, as well as another building that was clearly a working garage. Tucked back further into the woods was more of the compound, but it was getting hard to see in the dark.

I rode with Molly to the Lair for two reasons. One, because parking was a problem, and two, because I didn't think my car could have made it up the hill. As pretty as it was, the Lair was like a fortress. Hard to get to, and once the heavy gate was locked, it would render the compound impenetrable.

As I walked into the lodge, I realized my expectations were way off. I was thinking it would be full of torn-up mismatched furniture, sticky floors, stale cigarette smoke, and the like. Instead it was rustic, charming, and clean. Very clean for a live-in clubhouse.

Molly gave me a quick tour. The main front room was a catch-all that spanned both floors, the second floor appearing more as a landing loft with a private apartment on one side and private rooms on the other. One of those was the conference room where the club officers and their guests would hold their biker church meetings. The other apartment side was the private residence and bedrooms for Brick and Betsey. The main room had wooden frame couches with Native American printed cushions. Homemade rectangular coffee tables covered in permanent sweat rings from so many beer bottles and glasses sat in front of the couches. Several big flat-screen TVs were mounted on the walls around the massive room; one in the side extension that held a pool table and a foosball table, and another in the bar area in the other side extension. The bar was smaller than the one at the River's Edge, but better stocked with higher-grade booze. There was a collection of neon beer lights glowing on the walls, and a couple of deer heads mounted. The one in the bar area sported a red cap, sunglasses, and had a cigarette dangling from its mouth.

A number of members were already at the Lair, hanging

out, shooting pool, playing video games. Some of them I'd met briefly, others I did not know at all. Donna was there, as well as Nikki and a few other women I'd seen around the bar but hadn't met. Everyone could be identified by either their cut, or lack of one. Those men not wearing a Dragon Runners cut were called hangarounds, and were hoping to prospect into the club. But just because you got a chance to attend a private party at the Lair didn't mean you automatically got to prospect. That was by invitation only, and Brick was very particular about who he let into this inner sanctum. I felt out of place, like a fish trying to swim in desert sand. I could tell this would be a long night, and my best bet was to become invisible and stay that way.

Led Zeppelin was playing from a fancy set of surround-sound speakers mounted on the walls when I walked in. Brick met me, his red-and-gray hair pulled back in a short ponytail and his bushy russet beard bristling. He was a bear of a man, large with a slight gut. His real name was Jesse Davis, but his fellow bikers knew him as Brick, both for his red hair and for his hard line when it came to the club and club business. The tattoo on his forearm was of a snake vaguely resembling a dragon, with the classic American motto "Don't Tread on Me."

"Betsey called about the kids. I talked to Blue, and he's on his way. The sheriff's letting him go off duty to get home and take care of business with the kids, but he's not gonna be here for a while. Thanks for covering. I owe you one."

This was the longest sentence he'd ever said to me. I swallowed and tried to hide my nervousness.

"No problem, Brick, I'm glad to help," I said as I took off my coat. "I'll take stock of the bar and handle it as best as I can."

Molly piped up, "I got a couple hours until I have to sit duty at the station. I'll help out until then and keep her sorted. The other old ladies here will pitch in as needed. We'll be fine. You get church started. The quicker that's done, the faster you can get to your grandkids."

Brick nodded and placed a hand on my shoulder, squeezing lightly. "You let me know if someone bothers you."

He left, tromping up the wooden L-shaped staircase to the loft area and the conference room. Taz, Stud, and Mute followed, along with the other members. The few bikers that were left immediately made a beeline for the bar.

For the next few hours, I was pouring beer and shots like crazy. I was amazed at the amount of booze they could drink. I mixed a few pitchers of margaritas, and those got sucked down almost as fast. The bikers that were not involved in the church meeting were loud, cussing hard and feeling up any woman who did not have on a "property of" vest. I saw Nikki in the corner making out with two men, one with his tongue down her throat and the other with his hand under her short skirt. Donna was straddling a thin, brown-haired biker, holding a shot glass between her breasts. He took it with his mouth, pulled it out, and tossed it back. She squealed and gyrated on his lap.

"Is it always like this?" I asked Molly. She was sitting at the bar along with Tambre, both of them there to offer me some protection from the horny bikers.

Molly took a swig of her Diet Coke. She was on duty later and couldn't drink. "No, it's not. See those guys over there at the PlayStation? Their cuts are a little different. Same club, but different chapter. They are on the Tennessee side. The ones shooting pool are from the West Virginia chapter. Something's been going on for a while, both here and at the other end of the Tail. Got a lot of meth that's being run through here, and more than once, someone claimed they saw bikers with Dragon Runner cuts involved in drug exchanges. Brick thinks someone is making counterfeit cuts to implicate the club. That's why this church meeting is happening. Brick invited the other chapter presidents here for a sit-down. The club has been clean for a long time now, but there are still some out there who don't like the change and want to go back to what it was when Jesse Jr. was running it."

Tambre hissed. "Molly, that's club business! You're not supposed to know *or* share!"

Molly hissed right back, "I work at the sheriff's office, Tam, how'm I not supposed to know? Any woman in this club needs to know something, if not for safety, but at least to be able to tell a real Dragon Runner from a fake one."

Tambre went silent and sucked down more of the margarita I'd made for her.

The night kept going, and the party atmosphere died down a bit. Tambre could only stay until ten when she had to go sit with her grandkids and Molly left around eleven to get to work. The church meeting had started around nine, and it was closing in on midnight. Everyone seemed occupied, either with video games, pool, darts, or making out with one of the club women. I'd seen several of them disappear from time to time, going to the back bedrooms. The sounds of fast pounding sex could be heard; Nikki was particularly loud.

No one had bothered me yet, and I hoped it stayed that way. One of the young club prospects had come down once from the conference room to take a tray of beers and shots to the meeting members, but no one else had come down. I had my invisibility on, and chanced coming out from behind the bar to gather up the empty shot glasses and beer mugs. Most of the bottles were hurled into a big gray rubber trash can in the far corner of the bar, however, a few of them missed, making a sticky mess on the floor of broken glass and beer dregs. No one had made an attempt to clean it up. I was sure if Betsey were behind the bar instead of me, she would've jumped down the culprits' throats and made them clean up their own mess, but because I was the one behind the bar, the mess stayed and got bigger.

I moved around the room, careful to stay out of the way and not attract any attention. I managed to get quite a few glasses gathered, and retreated back to the bar. Donna was curled up on one couch, half on a visiting member's lap. He was leaning back, his eyes half-closed while she rubbed at his erection through his jeans. It wouldn't be long before she would lead him to the back rooms. I hurried through and set up a load in the dishwasher, then pressed my luck by tackling the mess in the corner.

I cleared the glass, swept, and mopped the area quickly. I was just thinking I was home free and could go hide behind the bar again, when a pair of hands grabbed me from behind and pulled me into a hard male body.

"Well, well, well! Look what the Kat dragged in!" Joker sang in my ear.

I froze for a moment and he took that opportunity to grind himself into my backside.

"Nice to see you again, Puh-puh-pussy Kat." He popped the *P* hard in my ear, and I felt the draft of his breath against my cheek.

I tried to pull away.

"Please let me go, Joker. I'm only here to fill in for Betsey," I said, trying to keep an even voice and hide my sudden nerves.

"Oh, but I don't want to, pretty kitty." He snaked his arm around me, trapping both of mine against my sides. "I wanna play. Come on, baby, let me pet that pussy." He reached around my front and shoved his hand between my legs, grabbing me hard. I gasped and tried to pull away again.

"Uh-uh, baby! Where you going?" he sang, sticking his face into the side of my neck and licking my skin. "Mmmm… tastes good. I bet that pussy tastes better. Can't wait to dive right in. I'm gonna eat that pussy raw, then I'm gonna fuck it so hard you'll be yowling at the moon for more."

"No… I don't…." I struggled for words. The wet feel of his tongue on my neck was nauseating.

"You ain't claimed and you're at the Lair. That means you're open for business. Come on, pretty pussy. I gotta room on loan in the back. Let's see how loud I can make you purr!"

He started dragging me towards the back hallway, and I had no choice but to shuffle along. I pulled at his vise-like grip, and could feel the panic rising in the back of my throat.

"Joker, I'm not kidding, I don't want this!"

"Yes, you do, Pussy Kat. You want to spread those legs wide for me," he stated in his singsong voice.

"Stop!" I yelled desperately, as loud as I could. Suddenly Joker was no longer at my back, and I lost my balance. A pair of strong arms caught me, and I looked up into Stud's furious eyes.

"You okay, Kat?" he asked in a low voice.

I was shaken up, but I wasn't hurt so I nodded. The thudding sound of flesh hitting flesh met my ears, and I heard the chant of "Fight, fight, fight" as well. I looked out in the middle of the main room to see Mute standing with his fists clenched, and Joker laid out on the floor, clutching a bloody nose.

"What the fuck!" he yelled, blood running down his twisted face. "I don't see no property tag on her! She fucking you, Mute? Or Stud?"

His eyes grew comically wide, and his mouth formed a large exaggerated O. "Oh! Oh! OH! I get it! You guys are sharing now! Well, fuck me!" He started laughing. The sound was disturbing given the blood and the maniacal look in his eyes. "Mute done found him a piece. When you done tapping that ass, I want a turn. Just like old times, eh?"

Mute reached down and grabbed the front of Joker's cut and hauled him to his feet, drawing back his fist for another punch.

"Whoa, whoa there, big fella!" Joker smiled, the blood creating a macabre mask. "You know me, I was just joking around!"

Mute didn't look like he was joking at all. He nailed Joker in the side of the jaw. Joker went down, more blood went flying, and more yelling sounded.

I tried to move out of Stud's arms to go stop the fight, but he held me back. "Stay put, baby girl. This has been a long time coming. It's not just about you."

Mute picked Joker up again. The bloody man was dazed, but still laughing crazily.

"Damn, Mute! You still pissed over Maya? That bitch is long gone!"

I could hear Mute's rage double in my head. I was afraid he would kill Joker, and while I didn't think I'd cry too hard at the funeral, the fallout Mute would face wasn't worth it.

"Stop them! Please!" I begged, my eyes filling with tears.

Stud looked at me with those fantastic blue eyes, and lightly shook his head.

"Mute had a woman years ago. Maya. Started out as a bunny, but hooked up with Mute real fast. He loved that bitch completely and he put his patch on her. Never saw him care about anyone like he did her. He took care of her, protected her, got her anything she wanted, thought she loved him back. She might have in her own way, but not enough to stay with him or stay faithful to him. Joker came through and charmed the pants off her, and I mean that in the literal sense. Mute caught them going at it in his room at the clubhouse. Joker was balls deep in her ass and she was high as a kite, wearing the cut he gave her that said Property of Mute. Not sure which is worse. A man seeing his woman shitting all over the patch he gave her, or the disrespect of a brother in making it happen.

"It took four of us to hold Mute back from beating the ever-lovin' shit outta both of them. Maybe even killing them. As mad as Mute can get, I've never seen rage like that, and I hope I never do again. Long story short, Mute took back his patch, which is an ugly divorce here in the club. Brick made Maya leave town, and made Joker go nomad. He wanted to take Joker's patch, but club rules say heritage members are exempt from just about everything. Joker would have to kill someone before he would be kicked out."

I took a gasping breath and tried to control my quivering lips. My heart bled for Mute's story. A betrayal like that would leave deep scars. Joker and Mute were supposed to be brothers, but how could one do that to the other?

A sonic wave blasted the room, the powerful noise coming from Brick.

"Enough!" he roared, coming down the stairs. "This is MY house! This is MY club! NO ONE DISRESPECTS ME HERE!"

Brick entered the fight ring that had formed around the two combatants. His face was flushed red and his two-hundred-fifty-pound frame shook with rage. He grabbed the front of Joker's cut and threw him to the ground. "Who the fuck do you think you are? This ain't no joke, asshole! You know the fucking rules of my fucking house!" He pointed to me, still being held by Stud. The hard authority that was Brick filled the room, and nobody could look away or speak. "Hear me now and hear me good, *all* y'all! That one is under *my* protection! You fuck with her, you fuck with me! And everyone here knows what happens when you FUCK WITH ME!"

Brick's powerful stare made everyone else's eyes drop. Mute went toe to toe with him for a moment longer, before he too was lowering his. "Party's over! Shut it down and get the fuck out!"

There was some general muttering, but the partiers left, going to their cabins and rooms, either as members or as guests.

"Donna! Nikki! You get them other bitches in here and clean up this fucking mess before you go. If you're staying with someone tonight, they can damn well wait! My fucking house comes fucking first!" Brick yelled, the rage still on his face.

Box was helping Joker to his feet. The bloody man was silent for once. Brick jerked his hand to the door.

"Get that motherfucker outta here! Brothers or not, you ain't welcome here no more! Mute, make sure they get all the way off Lair property. I don't wanna see nothing but their fuckin' taillights in the distance."

He turned to Stud. "You claimin' her?" he growled, his bushy eyebrows beetled up. Mute froze on his way out the door and turned back to Brick, his expression tight and unreadable.

"No, but I'll throw down for her," Stud answered calmly.

I was startled to hear his answer. What did he mean? Throw down for me? Claiming? I was not well versed in biker language. I had no idea what any of this meant. Both Stud and Mute came to rescue me, but was that the same thing as claiming? Did I want to be claimed by one of them? Was claiming the same as patching? If it was, I didn't want that! I looked at Mute, still as silent in my head as he was in real life. He was staring hard at Stud. I prayed at that moment to whoever could hear me for invisibility.

"Then let her the fuck go." Brick's voice was lower but no less commanding. "She ain't staying with you tonight. She's gonna take the extra room in my and Betsey's suite. Tired of watching you fuckers! One a y'all's got to shit or get off the pot!"

Mute turned angrily and left the house to finish clearing the property. As he stomped out of the lodge, he grabbed a bottle of whiskey by the neck, tipped it back, and took several swallows straight. I'd never seen him drink anything but coffee at the bar, and was a bit shocked at the ease with which he let the fiery liquor go down his throat. I wasn't sure that a drunk Mute was better than a sober one.

Stud stiffened but released me and stood back. "Wait here, and I'll get you that toothbrush and a tee to sleep in."

He left the room, leaving me standing there with Brick.

"I'm so, so sorry, Brick," I stammered, my arms hugging my middle, instinctively trying to get smaller. "I d-didn't mean to cause trouble. I... um... I just wanted to help you and B-B-Betsey!"

My throat was closing up and I was losing the fight with my tears. A sob broke out of my mouth and I clamped my hand over my lips, desperately trying to hold in the rest.

Brick softened up immediately into the teddy bear I'd always thought he was. "Come 'ere, darlin'. Ain't your fault," he crooned, hugging my shaking form into his barrel chest. "This ain't the way my house runs, and I'm sorry you saw it this way. Don't matter if a woman is an old lady, claimed, or open to the public, she's in my house, she's safe. She don't gotta do nothing she don't want to do."

He stroked my back as I stifled more sobs. He was the patriarch of the club family as well as his own. *This is what it feels like to have a father look out for you.* A fresh wave of tears threatened to spill, and I struggled to fight them back.

"Anyone comes in my house, needs to show respect. For me, for my club, for my rules, for my brothers, for my women. I don't get that, then you don't come in my house. Simple as that."

I heard Donna, Nikki, and the two other club women moving around the room clearing and cleaning a bit. I knew they could hear Brick talking to me, but I couldn't see them. I felt someone else come up to us, but I couldn't tell if it was Stud or Mute.

Brick kept talking, his growly voice low and soothing, "My rules are simple too. Drink and party as much as you want, but stay in control enough you don't trash my place. I worked too hard and gave too much to build it for some drunk fuckers to tear it up. Fuck whoever you want and whenever, but take it to a room. Have that respect for your woman even if it's for one night, and have respect for other club old ladies not to throw that in their faces. Betsey don't like seeing that shit. And if your woman says no, respect that too and move on to someone else."

Brick pulled back from me, letting me go, but he put his hands on my shoulders and looked me directly in the eye. His face was serious and I couldn't look away.

"Betsey had a bad past with a drug runner, almost got herself killed over it. A woman needs to feel safe in her own place, and she went through something no woman should ever have to go through. This is her safe place now, and I make sure it stays that way. She don't allow no drugs in here, not even pot. Boys wanna smoke one, they go to the cabins. She don't even like cigarettes much, so the boys take that outside too. They respect my old lady enough to give her that. In turn, she takes care of them, their women, and the club. You keep helping and respecting her, you always gotta place here. You also got my protection."

Brick dropped his hands, and I spotted Mute coming in the front door. Donna stopped what she was doing and went over to him, making sympathetic noises and pressing against his arm. His face was still tight and he held his body rigidly, as if he was full of energy that had no outlet.

Stud chose that moment to hand me a toothbrush still in the package and a faded Harley T-shirt. "Here you go, baby girl. You need something, my room is down the back hall, last room on the right. You go get settled. It's after midnight, so we'll deal with what we need to tomorrow." He pressed his lips against my forehead and pushed me toward the steps after Brick's retreating form.

I took one last look at Mute's impassive face before going upstairs. My mind was numb, and the need to retreat was great. Brick showed me to a plain but nice room with a small adjoining bathroom. The apartment side of the loft was bigger than I thought, and really nice. I showered, used the lotions there for guest use, and opened the new toothbrush Stud had given me. His T-shirt was old and big. It hung down to mid-thigh on me. I got in the queen-size bed and tried to sleep, but was too keyed up. Restless, like I'd seen Mute earlier. I fidgeted and flipped for what seemed like hours, my mind wrestling with thoughts of Mute and Stud.

Claiming? Patching? Did one of them really like me like that? Plain old invisible me? Was that possible?

I finally got out of the bed, intending on slipping quietly to the bar and grabbing a shot of something that might help me relax enough to sleep. I slipped on my jeans, left the bedroom, and tiptoed my way through the suite. I heard Brick snoring loud enough to wake the dead in his own room, so I felt safe enough that I could sneak downstairs and get back quickly. I got to the loft, and heard another noise. I looked over the railing and almost went to my knees in shock. There was just enough light to show Donna bent over the pool table, completely naked, and a shirtless Mute pumping into her from behind.

The half-empty whiskey bottle sat on the green felt next

to her. His pants were lowered just enough to allow him access. She was gasping and moaning with each hard thrust, and he held her hips, pulling her back into his body. The rhythmic slap of flesh on flesh echoed in the large room. I stood there and watched. I should have been disgusted or embarrassed. I should have turned away, but I couldn't move. I was mesmerized by the sight of Mute's flexing tattooed muscles, the silver chain around his neck glinting in the bluish moonlight. This was raw, almost brutal sex. Not even sex.

This was fucking.

Donna was clawing at the table and gasping. He grabbed her arms, forcing them to her back, and pounded inside her. Donna screamed her climax, helpless as Mute kept going. He threw back his head, eyes closed, driving harder, and I felt my own sex pulse at the sight. His neck corded up as he clenched his jaw. I watched as he reached his own release silently, thrusting one last time deep into Donna's body.

I was not a virgin, nor was I opposed to sex, but it had never been a big nor steady part of my life. It also had never been the supposed mind-blowing experience other women seem to enjoy. My one boyfriend whom I'd had years ago introduced me to it, and after that first painful night, it didn't seem to me it was all it was cracked up to be. For the few months we stayed together, I let him do what he wanted, when he wanted. It didn't do much for me, but it kept him happy for a while. Then he complained I didn't participate enough. That I was cold in bed. He broke up with me using the clichéd "it's not you, it's me" line, but I knew he really meant it was me.

This is why I was shocked to feel so turned on as I gazed at the sight below. I wanted it to be *me* there on the pool table, him holding *me* down, driving into *me*, making *me* come. There was also a pain in my chest knowing I had the answers to my questions. It would never happen. Mute only tolerated my presence for what I could do for the club and Betsey; otherwise, he had nothing to do with me. He would rather fuck a club bunny than be with me.

I watched as he pulled out. He removed the condom, tied a knot in the end, and threw it in the closest trash can. Donna cooed and made a big show of rolling off the table. I couldn't hear was she was saying. I just watched as she pressed herself against Mute while he wiped off and tucked himself back in his pants. Running her hands up and down his chest, she kissed and licked him, sucking at his nipples.

He stood there still as a statue, watching her touch him. He didn't touch her back, hold her in his arms, or kiss her. Instead, he looked up at the balcony railing, right into my eyes, like he knew I'd been there the whole time and the fucking scene was nothing more than a show for my benefit. I felt a sob crawl up the back of my throat. His face was hard. His mouth set in a grim line. His eyes dead.

"You should leave," I heard him in my head. *"You don't belong here."*

He pushed Donna's grasping hands off him, picked up the whiskey bottle, and turned to walk out of the house. She cried out after him and tried to follow, but he ignored her and continued through the door. The naked woman crumpled on the floor in a curled-up heap. I could hear her crying out her hurt. I knew how she felt, but I jammed the heel of my hand against my mouth to stifle my own sounds. Brick was still snoring from his room in the suite, ignorant of my movements.

I went back to the guest room, climbed in the bed, and hugged one of the big, fluffy pillows to my middle. I buried my face in another one and let loose just a little, soaking it with the flood of tears I'd been holding back. Miraculously, after that little crying jag, I felt a great relief, almost giddy. I would do what I did best. I would lock my feelings and hurts into a corner of my mind and leave them there. I had a plan. Finish school, start working at the hospital full-time, save up some money, and move somewhere else. I would stick with it. I would ignore Mute, and do my job, period. I would wrap myself in a Harry Potter cloak of invisibility, and I would survive. With my mind clear, I was finally able to fall asleep.

***

Mute sat on one of several picnic tables that were scattered around the club's courtyard. It was a cool night, but he was drunk enough not to feel it. All around him were the sounds of the woods. He tipped back the whiskey bottle, and swallowed the last of the strong liquor. It burned a welcome path to his stomach. He went to throw the bottle across the yard, but was sober enough to know Betsey would have his hide if she came back to a courtyard with broken glass in it. That woman ran a tight ship, both at the bar and at the clubhouse. He set the bottle down next to him, burped lightly, and listened to the crickets and katydids chirping and buzzing.

Fucking Joker! Goddamn cocksucker! If he wasn't a brother, he needs to be taken up the mountain!

He glanced back at the lodge. *Bet she'll leave now.*

Sometime during his whiskey binge, he had come back into the lodge. Donna had followed him, chattering, touching, and rubbing. He didn't remember her words to him, as he didn't spend a lot of time paying attention to her. He found her annoying most of the time, and her constant pursuit of him was irritating to say the least.

But tonight he was drunk and she was available. The minute she opened his jeans and pulled out his dick, he gave in and plowed into her on the pool table in the main room. He knew he was using her only to get off, his head full of Kat while he was pounding into her body, and now he was regretting it. Even if Donna was a club bunny, still didn't make it right to be fucking her while he was wishing it was someone else.

When he spotted Kat watching, he was thrilled that perhaps she would see how much she didn't belong in club life, almost happy.

Fuck! he thought again. If he was so happy about it, then why did he feel like shit?

CHAPTER SEVEN

The day of the Dragon Runners' Halloween barbecue was as perfect as a fall day in the mountains could get. The sun was high and bright in a clear, vivid blue sky. The trees were bursting with earthy colors, and the campground where the event was held was full of people, both biker and townsfolk. The crafters were out selling a year's worth of handmade wares. Screaming and laughing children ran through the games area, some sporting face paint and carrying plastic prizes. The woody, mouthwatering scent of roasting meats came from a line of massive black smokers that had been set up at the pavilion picnic area.

Betsey had everything running like clockwork. Four men were manning the smokers that had been going since before dawn. Paper plates, plastic cutlery, and napkins, all in massive boxes, were set out and ready to go. More than twenty large coolers lined the tops of the picnic tables, storing any dishes that people brought to share in the potluck, one side for cold and the other for hot. My task was to greet those who brought in food, put a label on the dish with their name so nothing got mixed up, and get it in either a hot cooler or a cold one. I had never thought to use a cooler to keep things hot, but it worked. Molly took in donated bags of Halloween candy for the trick-or-treaters who would come through the tents and cabins at dusk. Tambre's job was to keep Betsey from panicking.

"I don't know!" Betsey exclaimed for the umpteenth time that morning. "Do we have enough barbecue? Ain't got time to start another hog. I should send over to Ingles and pick up some readymade."

Tambre sighed and repeated for the umpteenth time that morning, "We're fine, Betsey! We got plenty, and every year we end up with enough leftovers to feed two more festivals. Ease up, sister! Everyone is happy! It's all good!"

Everyone was happy, even me. Mute and I had settled into another truce, hopefully one that would last. He didn't communicate directly with me unless he had to, but he still had this urge to look out for me. I'd worked the Lair several times since the night I saw him and Donna together, but no one bothered me for anything more than friendly flirting. Brick's edict had done its job, and Mute acted like a bodyguard, his burning gaze cutting down anyone who got too close. Stud talked with me a lot at the Lair and would make sure I had what I needed should I have to spend the night in the room that was now known as mine. Usually he'd lend me a tee even though I brought a few of my own.

"Get that damn thing outta here!" Betsey's yell cut through my thoughts. Brick had ridden up to the pavilion cover and the roaring from his bike was deafening.

"When's the food gonna be ready, woman?" he yelled back with equal volume. "Been working all morning, running kids up and down the Tail. You need to feed your man!" He winked at us. Clearly, he enjoyed riling up his old lady.

"I'll feed him a knuckle sammich if he don't get outta my face! Q's ready now, just gotta get it pulled off. You can announce the blessing and get 'em started. I need to... Brick!" she squealed.

He enveloped her in a bear hug and made rapid smacking noises with his mouth against her neck. She laughed and pretended to struggle to get away from him.

"Stop it, you horny old goat! I got stuff to do!"

"Mmmm... best damn woman in the state. Love you, baby."

"Love you too, darlin'. Now get the hell outta my way!"

He left with a roar of laughter and the thunder of his bike.

The club brothers were working various jobs around the campground. The prospects got the lower ones, like emptying trash cans and making sure the camp bathrooms were stocked with toilet paper and soap. Some were regulating the games, and most of the senior members were taking the kids on motorcycle rides on a short Tail run. I'd seen Brick, Taz, Stud, and Mute with kids on the backs of their bikes. Only kids that were twelve years old and older could ride, and they had to wear helmets that made their heads look four times bigger than their bodies. No helmet, no bike ride. Mute took the older kids, as communication was a safety issue. Mute could hear the kids on the helmet mics, but could only communicate back with hand signals. This could have been a major frustration for him, but he seemed to handle it well. I was actually pretty impressed with his patience and easy demeanor in the few glimpses I got of him with a starry-eyed and excited teenager on the back of his bike. This was not the Mute I knew at the bar.

Brick announced the blessing through the campground PA system. It was nice to see no one argued or got offended, or even if they did, no one said anything. The people bowed their heads and the men removed their hats.

For the next few hours, Betsey, Tambre, Molly, and I helped control the chaos that happened around the food tents and picnic areas. It was self-serve, but we four kept up with replenishing the food platters, drink coolers, checked beer kegs, filled napkin dispensers, kept the food lines in order and moving, helped a few people who were in wheelchairs, and handled anything else that came up. I was exhausted by the time most of the mass of people had come through the lines, but I was also ecstatic and happy. I'd been a needed part of a well-oiled machine, and I was thrilled to be included. I was treated like I belonged there. This was my place, where I fit in. The townsfolk greeted me as if I was a part of the club. They smiled and nodded, some calling me by name, remembering me from the bar.

"Hey, Kat, how's school?"

"It's going well, should be done soon."

"Still gonna work at Mute's place when you're done?"

Mute's place?

"I don't know yet. Depends on when I get hired and where my forever job will be."

"Kat! Get your butt over here and get some food!" I heard Betsey holler, unintentionally rescuing me.

The hickory smoke flavor of the barbecue was fantastic. There was a plethora of vegetable dishes, casseroles, breads, deviled eggs, and salads, with just as many cakes, pies, and other desserts sitting on the groaning tables.

The riders took a break from running the kids and joined everyone at the picnic table that was reserved for club members. Brick, Taz, Mute, Cutter, and Stud came and sat with us as we women chatted about the next round of work and the ride that was coming up later in the afternoon. Stud sat down next to me with a piled-up plate of food. Brick and Taz sat across from me, next to Betsey and Tambre. Cutter sat on the other side of Molly, and Mute sat down next to Brick, not quite in my line of sight but still across from me. The noise of the world shrank as they surrounded us in quiet protection. The sense of belonging to this fantastic group of people was stronger than ever, something I'd never had before in my life and now found myself needing.

Brick was talking between bites of food. "Good thing we sent Dodge and Bruiser up here last week. Some asshole decided he needed firewood and started taking pieces of the pavilion for it. They said it looked like an ax was used. Only reason it's still up is the framework is all metal poles and pipe. I bet that fucker felt it good when he swung in and hit steel."

The people around him laughed and shook their heads. He loaded up his fork and continued, "The prospects will do a trash run at five and take the bulk of it to the landfill, otherwise them dumpsters will be overflowing. They'll come hose down everything tomorrow when the pavilion is empty. No use doin' it today. Community house needs to stay open late."

He rambled off several other comments and orders. I felt myself fading away from the conversation and lapsing into a food coma. I was ready to pop from being so full, and my mind was drifting so much I didn't realize when I started leaning into the warm body next to me until an arm wrapped around me and pulled me into it. I startled awake and looked up into Stud's amused face.

"So what do you say, baby girl?"

"Sorry… um… what?" I stuttered, coming fully awake.

Molly chimed in, "Just say yes, Kat. You'll have a blast!!"

"Yes?" I answered. "To what?"

"The fun run, sleepyhead! Stud said you can ride with him."

The fun run was the final one of the day when the members ran the Tail just for themselves. It was a show of brotherhood, but instead of cuts and colors, everyone wore costumes. Old ladies were included, as well as any other invited women. Not everyone got to go on the fun run, and I understood it was a big deal to be a part of it. "I've never ridden on the back of a motorcycle before. Is it hard to do?" I asked.

ML NYSTROM

"Nope, just gotta get a good grip and hang on tight," Stud answered with his arm still around me. "I won't let anything happen to you."

I glanced up at Mute. His face was blank, but he was looking into my eyes with a direct stare.

What else can I say? "I guess I could do that."

"Great!" Molly chirped. "We'll finish up here, get changed at the cabin, and meet back up here around five thirty. Y'all get going! We've got stuff to do."

The men were quickly shooed off, and we four went to the club's reserved cabin where I found out what "get changed" meant. This was the ultimate in girl time—it looked like Tambre's beauty shop had exploded. Both Molly and Tambre ignored my protests and in no time at all, my hair was up in a halo of hot rollers. Betsey had brought in a bottle of tequila and four shot glasses. She pressed one in my hand.

"Bottoms up, ladies!" she exclaimed, before slinging the liquor back. All of us followed her lead. The burn took my breath away, but I managed to down it without choking.

"Trust us! You'll like it!" Molly was having fun playing with her grown-up doll, and Tambre was enjoying working with my hair as well. Betsey sat back, her own hair up in hot rollers, adding to the fun comments. She poured another round of shots for us, and in true Betsey form, filled the air with words.

"You got two of my boys dangling and you don't even know it, do you?"

"Huh?" I said, holding my head still while Tambre

86

worked her magic. "What are you talking about, Betsey?"

"Stud and Mute, girlfriend!" she said, picking up a bottle of fire-engine-red nail polish. "Them boys is both hot for you. Cain't you tell?"

Stud I could maybe see, as he'd been so nice to me, but he'd never touched me in any other way than friendship. Mute? Definitely not, after watching him with Donna.

I burst into laughter, mostly to cover up my discomfort on the subject. "Mute's not interested in me, Betsey! He can barely stand to be around me! And Stud's just being nice."

"One of them will have to make a move soon, especially when they see you in your costume tonight! Voilà, baby!"

Molly whipped out a shiny black stretchy something, along with a mask and headband. "I'm… ah… oh my," I stuttered. Betsey handed me a third shot. Or was it the fourth? It was getting easier and easier to toss them back.

The cat suit was one piece, fitted tightly to my body, hugging every curve and leaving nothing to the imagination. It was like being naked in public. Molly had also made a black mask, tail, and ear headband to go with it.

"Go put it on! I wanna do your makeup next!"

Molly was practically frothing. I really didn't want to put that suit on, but Molly had worked hard to make it and I didn't want to spoil the night for her. I went into the only other room and wrestled myself into the tight suit. The material looked like leather, but stretched like spandex. It smoothed over my skin, showing off my hourglass figure. It made me look sleek, mysterious, and sexy. I found myself liking it, liking the feeling of being a desirable woman. The mask added a bit of ambiguity, and I could pretend to be somewhat invisible in it, but I was sure it was obvious who was in the costume. I'd thought I would be uncomfortable in something that showy, but I found myself looking forward to being seen in it. Of course, I was also a little drunk, so maybe the warm stirring in my gut was really the alcohol.

We walked as a group to the staging area where the bikers were preparing for the final run of the day. The kids were already trick-or-treating from tent to tent and trunk to trunk, and families were settling down. The scent of campfires wafted on the slight breeze. It was peaceful.

Betsey was dressed up as a devil woman, Tambre was supposed to be the goddess Hera in her Greek toga, Molly was a sexy witch in purple, black, and green, and I was her cat. We were treated like royalty, people calling out their thanks for a great day and for the food. I smiled as well, greeting people and accepting their gratitude as if I was a part of this biker family.

Betsey ran up to Brick as he whistled at her sexy devil costume. He himself was dressed as a matching devil with pitchfork, long red cape flying out behind him. Taz was in a Greek toga as Zeus, and he greeted Tambre with a warm hug. Molly took a flying leap on Cutter, who was in a purple-caped warlock costume. Stud was dressed as Thor, and he very much looked the part of a Viking god. He also sported a red cape that draped behind him, and fake hammer that dangled from his belt. His eyes glittered when he saw me.

"Are you sure you want to go on this ride with me, Kat? The way you look, I may not stop until we get to Vegas. You look fantastic."

I felt myself blush at the compliment, but also preened just a little. Having this man's attention was as intoxicating as the booze from earlier. "Thanks, Stud."

A harsh bike rev cut through the air, and I glanced over to see Mute. I lost my breath. He looked like the Phantom of the Opera dressed all in black. Tight pants tucked into cuffed leather boots, a loose shirt that laced at the front and was tied with a black sash. Black gloves covered his hands, and a black half-mask covered his face. I felt his eyes glare at me through the holes. Mackie was standing behind him, two helmets in his one hand. Apparently, Donna was not riding with Mute.

"I think I just died and went to heaven!" the older man declared, grabbing his chest and nearly dropping the headgear. "I get to ride and look at a beautiful woman all on the same day! God must love me!"

I laughed at his antics. He was one of my favorite people, always happy and free with his humor. He was one of the first people to accept me into the club family. Even though he didn't wear a cut, he was a big part of it.

"Mount up!" Brick yelled, and I turned back to Stud. He handed me a full helmet and face shield.

"You'll have to remove the cat ears, baby girl. A helmet is a necessary evil. I wouldn't want anything to happen to that pretty head of yours." He ran his hand through my hair, taking the ears with him, and his eyes got intense. I felt a flutter through my middle. This touch was more than friendly. I wasn't sure how to handle it, and my first instinct was to run. My second was to revel in it. I decided it was the booze talking. No way would this be real if I was completely sober.

He popped the helmet on my head and hooked the straps, then explained how to get on the bike behind him. I got on and tentatively put my hands on his waist, gripping lightly. He chuckled while putting on his own helmet.

"You're gonna need a better grip, baby girl. Pull up closer. I need to feel you at my back. This ride can get a bit cold, so snuggle tight and I'll keep you warm."

He pulled me up until I was pressed fully against him, my breasts crushed into his back, my arms wrapped tight around his middle. I could feel his muscles working as he shifted around on the bike, and the flutter in my middle grew. I was attracted to Stud, but men like him usually weren't attracted to me. He was smart, insanely handsome, super masculine, and I was—well, I was just me. It was scary to want more than friendship.

When he started the flaming machine we sat on, I could feel it through my entire body. The powerful vibration did something to me. The bike was like a beast coming alive, and I could feel it purring underneath me. It sent its message of acceptance through me, and the flutter in my middle turned into an ache. I could feel the place between my legs tingle, and wanted nothing more than to press down into the rumbling seat. My nipples hardened into little points where they were pressed into Stud's back. He must have felt them, as he placed one hand on my clenched ones and stroked my fingers. I groaned a little, more turned on than I had ever been before.

"Hang on, baby girl," I dreamily heard Stud say to me. "We're gonna have a good ride tonight."

I pondered for a split second if he meant a different kind of ride, then he took off and I could think of nothing else.

It was stunning. Scary. Exhilarating. The wind was cold as it rushed around me, and I was glad for the helmet's face shield. The bikes spread out as the Dragon Runners club opened up and flew. Stud pulled out ahead of everyone and ramped up his speed. We took the first curve on the Tail and I felt the inertia of the turn in my head and gut. The man and the bike worked as one, dancing over the road. I could feel the pressure of each curve, followed by a floating sensation as we prepared for the next, and then pressure again in the opposite direction. The powerful beast between my legs, the cold wind, the warm man I clung to, it was too much, and a need rose up in me that I hadn't paid attention to in a long time. I wanted this. I wanted to be a part of this so bad.

I groaned again at one particularly hard curve, and clutched at Stud's middle. He let go of one hand grip and stroked my hands again, caressing me. I was starting to believe it could be possible. That this man was truly interested in me. That later tonight I would have an experience I'd never really had before. Was I ready for this? Did I trust it?

I didn't get to answer that question, because at the next curve a deer ran out in front of the bike, followed by two more. The headlight made their eyes flash gold as they bounded across the asphalt. I heard Stud curse, and he swerved to avoid them. The bike skidded dangerously close to the edge of the road and he tried to compensate, but the force was too much and we were thrown.

I screamed as we flew off, the bike going one way and us going the other. Somehow Stud managed to grab me before we hit the ground, and rolled so his body was between mine and the ground. We came up hard against a tree, and I heard Stud curse loudly in pain.

"Goddammit!"

It got still and quiet now that the bike wasn't running. Only the faint buzz of the forest penetrated the helmet. I was lying next to Stud as he rested against the tree. Both of us were breathing hard. Whatever liquor-induced state I'd been in earlier was gone. I was stone-cold sober. Stud was in pain, I could hear it in his voice.

"You okay, baby girl?" he wheezed.

"I think so. Nothing broken. You?" I gasped.

"My arm. Definitely broke. I felt it crack. Goddamn deer!" he spat, not moving.

The rumble of other motorcycles came closer, and a few minutes later, Taz and Mute were sliding down the short embankment to us. I could see Tambre and Mackie peering over the side.

"Anyone hurt?" Taz asked in a deep growl. Mute bent over and gently pulled the helmet off my head. He started running his hands over me, feeling my arms and legs. I was in too much shock from the accident to think much about it.

"Broke my fucking arm. Think I turned my ankle too. Kat says she's okay. Probably banged up. She'll feel it tomorrow," Stud managed to say, biting off his words. "Fucking damn deer herd in the road! How's my bike?"

"Gonna need some paint; rest of it is okay far as I can tell. Laid it down good so the frame isn't bent, maybe the front wheel just a bit but could be worse. Mute, you get Kat up the hill. Flag the cage down. Should be here in a few minutes. Then come help me get Mr. Show-off here up the hill. Looks like the rest of our run is to the hospital."

Mute scooped me up and I automatically put my arms around his neck. I yelped at the sharp pain in my side and back. He stopped and looked at me, his teeth grinding and eyes glittering.

"Where are you hurt?" I could hear him asking.

"I don't think I broke anything, just bruised. Stud's the one who's really hurt."

He climbed up the steep hill and set me down gently. Mackie shuffled over and awkwardly sat next to me. Tambre stood on the other side, watching for the truck.

"How's your head, sweetheart? Dizzy? Seeing double?" she asked quietly. She had a small first aid kit in her hands and was rummaging through it.

"No, I'm good. Just shaky."

"Quite a spill. Y'all were lucky. Coulda been worse. A lot worse. There's people that don't get to walk away from a wreck on the Tail," Mackie intoned.

I could see Mute's jaw working in the fading light. He was agitated, his movements jerky as he moved Stud's torn-up bike from the road and made his way back down to the waiting men. Mackie kept talking about other accidents, how to drive a motorcycle, the habits of deer, and other trivial stuff I didn't pay much attention to. My mind was fully occupied with my own thoughts as the truck pulled up. Mute and Taz appeared on either side of Stud as they slowly made their way over the embankment. Stud's mouth was tight with pain as he hobbled along, his good arm around Mute's shoulders, his other arm cradled against his chest. Blood was on his shirt from several scrapes. I cringed as I realized he'd let himself get hurt in order to protect me.

I wasn't sure what to do. I tried to get up and help, but Mackie put his hand on my shoulder and pushed me back down.

"No, no, sweetheart, you stay put. You're full of adrenaline right now and can't feel if something else is wrong just yet. Let the boys handle things and you just be still." I stayed put.

Taz sorted everyone and gave out orders.

"Get the bike loaded and get Stud in the truck. It's faster to get to the hospital from here instead of going back to the campground. Tambre and I will follow the truck. I'll call Brick and let him know what happened. We're taking care of it and he can finish the run, but he'll have my ass if I wait to tell him."

He turned to Mute. "Mackie was supposed to ride back in the truck, 'cause he can only ride so long before it gets too much for him. That ain't changed. I'm putting him in the truck to go to the hospital with Stud and the two prospects. Ain't enough room for Kat, unless one of the others rides in the back with the bikes."

He looked at me and jammed a hand over his craggy face. "Kat, I know it's a lot to ask, but are you good to ride on a bike to the hospital? Mute will bring you, and we'll get you patched up. If you can't, you say so. Ain't no shame or problem, but that means Mute will stay here with you until I can get someone back here with a truck. Might take some time. You're studyin' to be a nurse, so you should know what's best and safest for you. You also know Stud's condition is the priority."

I had a lot of scratches. A few were deep and bleeding, but not serious. My ribs were hurting, but I could breathe okay. Nothing felt broken. I was shaking with adrenaline and knew I would crash sometime soon, and tomorrow I'd be incredibly sore, but there was nothing that would be a problem with me getting back on the bike. I just didn't want to get on the bike with Mute. He was glaring at me and breathing hard. I could tell he blamed me for this fiasco.

Even though it would bring me in close physical proximity to him, riding to the hospital on the back of his bike would be the fastest way to get out of his company and also not be alone with him for an extended period of time.

"I'm fine, I can ride." My voice was surprisingly steady. I was shaking like a leaf and clutching myself hard to control it. I really wanted to go invisible, become the incredible shrinking woman and disappear. But at this time, other people were more important.

"Stud needs his arm stabilized as much as possible. Is there something we can wrap around it? If no one has taken off the boot at his ankle, you should do that now before the ankle swells up so much you can't get it off later."

"Already done," Tambre said calmly, walking up to us and bringing my dented, scratched-up helmet with her. She smiled with classic serenity. I'd always thought Taz and Tambre were an odd couple, him being so rough and she being this quiet, sweet angel, but it was very obvious after a while how devoted they were to each other. "I'm not a nurse, but I've had a lifetime of patching up my four boys, this old man, and lot of others in the club. Even when you're careful, accidents happen."

She looked deep in my eyes and took my hands. "Tonight was just that, an accident. Wasn't your fault, wasn't Stud's fault, so don't go thinking it was something either of you did. Best we can do is take care of business. Yeah?"

"I'm good, Tambre, and thank you," I replied.

"Alrighty, let's get rolling!" Taz called out.

I put the helmet on my head and eased over to where Mute sat on his bike. It was bigger than Stud's, the growl deeper. I thought of Stud's bike as a beast, while Mute's bike was a predator. He didn't look at me as I painfully climbed on, lightly gripping his shoulder. His jaw was clenching and unclenching, his mouth thin and tight. He hated having to do this, but he would for Mackie and Stud. He was bigger than Stud, harder, and I hesitated putting my arms around him, only gripping his waist. He all but growled as he grabbed my hands and pulled me into his back, wrapping my arms around his waist and folding my hands together. He roared off, and I clutched at him to keep my place.

I was pressed into him like I was Stud earlier, and I

couldn't help but compare the two of them. Mute was bigger, harder, and rougher. Heat poured from his back, and I found myself snuggling into him, taking that comfort as the cold night wind blew around us. Stud controlled his bike like he was riding a horse, smooth and easy, shifting with just a touch. Mute rode like the bike was a part of him, like they were one unit instead of two. I could feel him move through the curves with barely a twitch. He didn't have to drive the bike as much as just ride it. I was starting to come down from the adrenaline boost and was crashing hard. Without thinking, I hugged him tighter and laid my head on his back, taking what I could from him, and hoping he wouldn't get pissed and throw me off the back.

My mind was drifting in that place between waking and sleeping, as the next thing I knew we were pulling up in front of the hospital emergency room. Stud was there, barely standing up with his good arm around Taz's shoulders, arguing with a nurse about sitting in a wheelchair. I was comfortable and groggy, so I didn't move very fast to get off the bike and away from Mute. Stud stopped his tirade when he saw me still curled up against Mute's back.

Mute let go of one of the handlebars, and for a moment covered my hands where they gripped his middle. Stud had made the same gesture earlier. Was there something I was missing? Stud saw it and got quiet. He abruptly sat in the wheelchair and gestured for the nurse to push him into the building. Mute helped me off, as my back was locked up tight.

A girl I knew from school, Jessica, was on duty tonight.

She was a cute, pixie-cut blonde, short and plump mother of two. Her husband did something for the railroad out of Dillsboro, but I wasn't sure what it was. She blinked owlishly when she saw me.

"Kat! Is that really you? What on earth? What are you wearing?"

"Long story, Jess." I groaned as Mute half helped, half carried me to the doors. Jessica rushed off to get another wheelchair, and put Stud and me through immediately with no detour into the waiting room. Halloween was typically a busy night at the ER, but either I avoided triage by being known, or the MC had priority.

Sometime later, I was out with several days' worth of sample painkillers and muscle relaxers, and another big bill to pay. I may have gotten first dibs at care, but nursing students didn't get discounts, unfortunately.

Mute apparently had already left to take Mackie home. Betsey was there waiting for me when I was wheeled out.

"Pssht! Slow down, darlin'. Here, let me help you up. You want your place? Guest rooms is all full at the clubhouse, but I can make room if you want to be there."

I eased into a standing position. "I'm good with my place. It's not that far. How's Stud? Mackie make it home okay?"

"Stud'll be back up at the clubhouse soon. He's getting hisself a nice cast on his arm and a fancy ankle boot. He'll be laid up a while for sure, and gettin' lots of attention from the girls. He ain't hurtin' with all them happy pills he got. You got some too, I see. Mute took Mackie home, and went to the Lair to help me out with something."

She loaded me in her Mustang and drove me to my apartment, making plans to have my car brought to me. "Prospects are cleaning up from the festival. I told them other club bitches to get to work as well. If they're gonna hang around the campground, they can help out too."

I stiffly got up the stairs with her help and into my apartment. Sheila and Chip were still out to wherever they go at night, and I was grateful I didn't have to deal with them. Betsey puttered in my small kitchen. I could hear water running as she filled a glass for me.

"You take a few days off to heal up, and then I'm gonna need you at the bar. Got a call from Blue. He got hit with some heavy mess last night, too. Had his kids last night at the festival, took 'em home, and found Jonelle out cold on the kitchen floor. He was at the hospital with her when they brought Stud in. Mute brought 'em to the clubhouse, so they're up in the guest room in our suite."

She rolled her eyes and hissed, "That stupid bitch needs to get her head on straight, or Blue needs to set her out permanently. Damn fool keeps takin' her back, swears it's part of his marriage vows. I'm glad he takes them promises seriously, but mark my words, one of these days, she's gonna really hurt someone."

I managed to get the ruined cat suit off and get into a nightshirt before painfully crawling into bed. Betsey handed me the water and two small white pills. I took them and eased back in the pillows.

"I'll be coming to work tomorrow night. I can't afford to

take time off, and frankly, it sounds like you can't afford me taking time either."

She ignored me.

"Brick's beside hisself over the accident. Stud's gonna be fine and you're gonna be fine, but too many other things been happening round the club businesses. More than he's letting on." She sighed. "I know somethin's going on between you, Stud, and Mute, and I won't pretend to know which direction you're supposed to go in. I bet you don't know either, but please, for right now, just let it play out. I love both them boys like they was my own, and I'd love to see you with either of them, but I will say this: Mute is one of a kind."

I was stunned. "I don't know about that, Betsey. I thought perhaps Stud might be interested in me earlier tonight, but I really think he's just a flirt with everyone. He's way out of my league, anyway. But you got Mute all wrong. He doesn't like me much and barely tolerates my presence."

"You'd be surprised, darlin'. Both them boys is tied up in knots over you. If you don't want either of them, you're gonna need to let them go."

The pills were kicking in and I was crashing hard.

"Do what you need to do, darlin'. I'll be back to check on you later." She patted my shoulder and left. I barely registered the sound of my bedroom door closing before I fell into a deep sleep.

* * *

Mute sat at the back bar watching Michelle and Cody play

some sort of racing game on the club's PlayStation. Their squeals of delight filled the lodge. Not many people were up, most of them already in their rooms or cabins for the night. A few were hanging around, shooting pool or sitting on the couches hanging out and recapping the day's excitement. Donna was there, still wearing a skimpy French maid outfit from earlier and sitting with Hammer, one of the newer club members. She was draped over his lap, her plumped breasts in his face. She knew the score, but she still sent him looks of longing.

Shit. He'd promised Betsey he'd keep an eye on the kids, but right now he was dying to go outside for a cigarette. He kept seeing in his mind's eye the sight of Kat bleeding on the side of the road. As far as a spill was concerned, it was not a bad one. It could've been far worse, yet when he repeated the scene in his head, he couldn't help his heart dropping through his stomach. He remembered how furious he had been when he saw what Kat had been wearing. If he were truthful to himself, he wasn't mad at her but rather how he'd reacted to it. One look at that tight body and he was struggling to keep his dick from getting hard. He had wanted nothing more than to go over to Stud's bike, punch his sworn brother right in the mouth, pluck Kat off the back, and put her on his own machine.

Mute shifted on the barstool, his lower body tightening. He'd had to fight his body's reaction earlier when he ran his hands over her, checking for injuries. He wanted to keep running his hands over her again and again, feeling the suppleness of her muscles and softness of her skin. He did get to put her on the back of his bike. When she wrapped herself around him, the aura around them balanced like she was supposed to be there.

Stud had come in and full of happy pain pills, grinning from ear to ear. Nikki had already decided to play nurse and was with him in his room. Mute snorted. Even if Stud was really interested in Kat for more than sex, he doubted the man could stop banging other women. Nikki was claiming she would be his old lady soon, but that was also unlikely, as he doubted she could stop banging other men. Every week Stud had a side piece or two from his fan club, and Kat hadn't caught on yet.

She don't deserve that, thought Mute as he looked unseeing at the TV. Michelle just won the racing game, and Cody was pouting. *Smart little girl. Kat is also smart. Too smart for this place. Too good.*

"What are y'all still doing up? Get yourselves upstairs and get to bed!" Betsey announced as she strode into the lodge. The two kids scrambled up the steps, giggling as they hurried. She walked over to Mute and set down her enormous purse on the bar counter.

"Long-ass night, eh?" she said, leaning against a barstool.

Mute didn't answer, trying to keep his face and thoughts neutral. He stood to go, his babysitting duties over for the night.

"She's gonna be fine, Mute," Betsey commented as she slipped off her high-heeled boots and stretched her toes. They cracked and popped, and she sighed at the relief. "Lord have mercy, what a day!"

Mute gritted his teeth, craving that cigarette more and more. Betsey was not ready to let it go just yet.

"She's a fine girl. Tougher than she looks! Smart. Works hard. Most reliable help the bar's had in a long time. Didn't think she'd hang with club life, but she's stuck around. Good for Mackie, too."

Mute refused to look at her, thinking it would encourage her to list more of Kat's best qualities. He agreed with some of what Betsey said, but still thought Kat was too soft. She was too kind, and this world had the potential to take that kind, chew it up, and spit it out. She needed to be protected from it even if that meant she left the club and went her own way. But if she did leave, who would protect her?

He needed to get out of there, grab a nicotine fix, and go for a long night ride. Maybe do a bit of patrol around the town. See if he could find a renegade drug dealer and beat the piss out of him. Mute nearly smiled. That would make him feel better for a while.

Betsey noticed the smile and gave one of her own. "Well, I'm off to bed. I got them hooligans of Blue's to take care of for the night. See you tomorrow, Mute. Keep them good thoughts, darlin'."

CHAPTER EIGHT

It was bitter cold, and snow was in the air with its heavy scent, ready to coat everything in white. Normally I liked winter weather, its crispness, the icicles decorating awnings and gutters, making everything sparkle, but right now not so much.

For weeks after the accident, I'd done my best to avoid both Stud and Mute. Stud was easy to avoid, as he spent most of his convalescence at the clubhouse doing the books. The few times I saw him when I worked the Lair, he had his arm in a cast and his foot propped up, being coddled by Nikki. He didn't seem to mind the attention and he seldom acknowledged my presence. Something had changed between us the night of the accident. That hurt, but I never did fully believe a man like Stud would ever go for someone like me.

Mute was harder to avoid, as I still had to work with him. I tried like hell to go invisible again, wearing my hair in its normal ponytail, dressing in plain jeans and T-shirts.

He was gruffer, surlier to me, and constantly in a bad mood when I was around. Even Mackie made comments about his attitude.

"Who the hell pissed in your corn flakes, boy?" he had blurted at Mute just a few nights ago. Mute had just looked at him and growled before stomping off.

"Damn ornery cuss needs a good fight! Get whatever shit is botherin' him out by pounding some flesh!" Mackie had muttered under his breath.

Normally, I can let things go, let them roll off my back. I'm good at it. Tonight, though, I was having trouble doing that. I'd been through several weeks of pure hell.

The timing could not have been any worse. My roommate had suddenly moved out several days ago by simply taking everything in the apartment and leaving me a note that she and her boyfriend were heading to California. Why, I didn't know. What I did know was when I said she took everything, I meant everything! My pitiful phone, my dishes, my furniture, even some of my clothes, including my good winter jacket. The reason I still had a laptop was because I'd had it with me for school work, otherwise she would've taken that as well. To top that off, I found out we were three months behind on rent. I had no idea what she had done with the money I'd given her for my half, just that the landlord had given me until the middle of December to move out. That was only a few days away, and I was flat-ass busted broke. I'd just paid my final tuition bill and had no money left to replace anything, and wouldn't have any for a few more weeks. The tips in my pocket would cover food for the next few days, but there was no way I had enough money to catch up rent, nor find a new place and pay for it. My anxiety level was high. I was trying to stay invisible, and trying to figure out where I was going to live, or at least stay until I could get back on my feet.

It was after my shift at River's Edge, pitch-black, and getting colder when I climbed into my car. I didn't have to work the Lair that evening, so I was planning on heading home while I still had one. I didn't have my jacket, and the heat hadn't worked in my faithful Fred for years. I shivered in the cold seat. Halfway to town, the engine sputtered and coughed. I began to beg, "Please, Fred, not now! Please get me home, and you can die later!" Fred didn't listen. He coughed a few more times, the headlights dimmed, and the engine died. With the car suddenly dead, the wheel became stiff, and I cursed as I wrestled the coasting car to the shoulder.

I turned the key and heard a clicking noise, then nothing.

"No, no, no, no!" I cried, begging the car to start just one last time. "Please, please, please!"

Fred made one valiant chug, and was silent. I banged my forehead on the steering wheel a few times and fought off the urge to scream. It wouldn't do any good. *Think, Kat, think.* I pulled open my wallet and counted the fifty some dollars I had from tips. There was a gas station a few miles down the road that might have an outside payphone. *Do those things even exist anymore?* I scrounged in the cup between the seats for a small handful of quarters, and prayed a phone was there in working order. A cab would probably eat up most of the cash I had, but what other choice did I have? Guess Ramen Noodles would be on the menu for a while longer.

I got out of the car, and the cold hit me hard, piercing straight through my clothes like a knife. The only jacket-like clothing I had left was a thin zip-up type. I wrapped it around me tighter, and took down my ponytail, letting my hair hang straight. That would warm my ears a bit. I locked the car and jammed my freezing hands deep in my pockets to ease some of the numbness already setting in. A few flakes of snow started to drift down. This was *not* going to be a fun walk.

I had barely taken the first step when a pair of headlights cut through the dark, and a huge black truck pulled up next to me. I was so cold, I didn't really care who it was until Mute stepped out with his perpetual scowl at me.

"What the hell are you doing?" his face told me.

"M-m-m-my c-c-car died," I chattered, my teeth clicking, "I th-think it's the b-b-battery."

Mute gestured for me to open the hood. He motioned for me to try the key, and frowned even deeper when he heard the click. Slamming the hood shut, he turned back to my shivering form and held up his hand, thumb and pinky sticking out to resemble a phone.

"I d-d-don't have o-o-one right n-n-n-now," I started, but he cut me off. His eyes bugged out at me and started gesturing wildly and angrily. I could hear him in my head.

"What the hell do you mean you don't have a phone right now? What the fuck happened to it? You're by yourself, it's

107

the middle of the night, and you work at a biker bar!"

He pointed at my car and flung his hands down at it. *"Your car is a fucking piece of shit, and even if it wasn't, you could've prevented it leaving you stranded by paying attention to it and getting it fucking serviced."*

I was getting colder and colder. The snow was falling faster now. My sinuses were tingling, and I fought back the tears as best as I could, but I was close to losing it. He moved closer to me and I stepped back, bumping into the icy frame of my car. He got in my face and kept at me, plucking at my thin jacket, flicking at my head, and jerking his hands in the air.

"You're not wearing a winter jacket, gloves, scarf, nothing! And you're gonna do what? Walk? In this kinda of cold? ARE YOU OUT OF YOUR FUCKING MIND?"

"Stop yelling at me!" I cried, and tried to shove him away from me. It was like shoving a brick wall. I fought it as best I could, but it was too much, I was too full. The accident, my being ignored, my invisibility, my fucking life, I spilled it all. I screamed and cried about my roommate stealing all my stuff, my tuition payments and lack of money, my soon-to-be homeless state—everything came out. My eyes were blinded by tears, my emotions raw and vulnerable. I had come to the end of my rope, and adding my now-dead car to the shit list that was my life was more than I could handle.

I gasped through my crying as I was enfolded in warmth. Mute had taken off his heavy leather jacket and draped it around my freezing body. Then he wrapped me in himself, pulling me close, pressing my face into his massive chest, surrounding me tightly with his strong arms, laying his head on top of mine. I was still crying and soaking his black Henley with my tears, but it was cathartic. The heat was wonderful, and I wanted to burrow deeper into him. A great sense of security washed through me, and gradually I was able to control my tears. I felt protected by his hard body, like he would both stand up for me and stand between me and danger. He was a man I could lean on, and let some of my load rest on his strong shoulders. I opened my arms and slid them around his waist, pressing as close as I could, and let his solid strength hold me and flow into me.

I'm not sure how long we stood in the cold, but at some point I became aware of him as a man. His hard body, heavy muscles, his masculine scent teasing my nose.

I heard a strange coughing sound, and felt him lightly jerking. It sounded like he was choking. I pulled back as far as I could to see if he was okay. His arms didn't loosen.

Mute's head was thrown back, mouth wide open, making that coughing sound. I could only stare. Mute was laughing. Laughing! This man I'd never ever seen crack a smile, was laughing! I was astounded.

Mute looked down at me, his mouth smiling and his eyes sparkling. He pointed to himself and quirked up one eyebrow. *"Me? Yelling?"*

I bit my bottom lip, not sure how to handle this side of the brutish man I had come to know.

"Well, you kinda were."

This set him off again, his hand moving to the back of my head, pressing me again into his chest. I smiled a bit and relaxed into him, amused myself at the unintended irony. Then it all changed.

He pulled me back just a bit and covered my mouth with his.

The shock I'd felt earlier when I saw him laughing was nothing to what I was feeling now. I could feel it from the top of my head through to the tips of my fingers and toes. For such a hard man, his lips were incredibly soft. He drew my bottom lip between his, sucked on it gently, and stroked it with his tongue. I moaned at the warm contact, and he took that as an invitation. He slanted his head a bit more, delving deeper into my mouth, stroking, exploring, and taking it leisurely. He tasted faintly of coffee, and all man. I would've expected him to be rougher, taking what he wanted the way he did with Donna. But with me in that moment, he was easy, gentle, and coaxing.

I let go and let it happen. I kissed him back. I no longer felt the cold night air. Instead I was on fire, my nipples hard where they pressed into him, and the place between my legs throbbing with sudden need. He growled in my mouth and I could feel the hunger in him. Hunger for *me*! I pulled at his shoulders, trying to get closer. His hands roamed to my lower back, and he pulled me tighter into his hips; the hard ridge of his erection pushed into my lower stomach was unmistakable. I squirmed against him, feeling his hardness.

He ended the kiss and pulled back slightly, his lips still close enough that I could feel his breath across mine. He nipped at my lower lip before releasing my mouth completely. I was trembling again, this time from want. I didn't know how to handle it, so I just stood there, wrapped in his arms, sharing breaths.

Then it was almost like it never happened. His face shuttered and settled back into its familiar scowl, and he abruptly let me go. If my lips weren't still tingling from his touch, I never would have known he'd kissed me. He pointed to his truck, telling me without words to get in.

"I need to get my laptop and stuff," I said, pulling his jacket off me to hand back to him. He pushed the jacket back to me, and held out his hand for my keys. I dumped them in his outstretched palm and he whipped his hand again toward the truck, scowling hard. I wasn't ready to call his jerk bluff. I turned and went to the truck, climbing in the passenger seat awkwardly. A moment later, he was yanking open the door and dumping my purse and computer on my lap. The door slammed hard, rocking the truck on its wheels. I buckled my belt, not sure of what to make of his sudden turnaround. He climbed in, fastened his belt, and started the truck with a low rumble. Heat poured from the vents, and I reveled in the toasty air. He fixed me with a piercing stare and quirked an eyebrow up in question.

"Where to?"

I gave him my address, and we drove through a shower of fluffy white snowflakes. I thought they were pretty as they sparkled in the beams from the headlights, but I didn't say anything. Gruff jerk Mute was back, and I expected him to simply drop me off and drive away. Instead he got out and followed me to the second-floor apartment, carrying my stuff for me.

"Thanks, Mute, but I'm good now. You don't have to stick around," I mumbled, struggling with my keys.

His response was to simply take the keys from my hand and open the door.

My apartment hadn't been much to begin with, and was basically nothing now. A single lamp lit the room, but nothing could hide its dingy bareness. There was only one room, besides the small bedrooms, that served as living room/kitchen and anything else it needed to be. Sheila had left the ratty couch covered in an old sheet, and an end table that had a broken, lopsided leg. My old box TV was gone, along with her CDs, her boyfriend's game system, and the rest of the mismatched furniture. The kitchen area was in one corner with a refrigerator, oven, sink, and a few cabinets. The cabinet doors didn't fit right and were hanging open, showing mostly bare shelves. She took the kitchen table and chairs, too.

I went into the small bedroom that was mine, Mute following me. I had a double bed, mattress only, that took up most of the floor space. There was a beat-up dresser, currently with its three drawers pulled out and empty, and a tiny, empty closet with no door. Still, I tried to make the best of what I had. My sheets and comforter were warm pastel colors of rose, gray, and blue. Luckily, Sheila's taste was more toward reds and blacks, so she left my bed alone, however she did take the small white rug that covered the hardwood floor. My bedroom lamp I'd found at the Goodwill store was small, made from white bumpy glass, and looked very feminine and antique. It sat on the lopsided folding chair I used as a nightstand. I'd draped a pink scarf across the top of the shade to give the room a bit of a glow. Mute stood in the doorway, his dark eyes looking around, taking it all in.

"I know it's not much," I started, sounding defensive even to my own ears. "But it's mine. I started out with nothing, and I can do it again."

His eyes met mine. I couldn't read him, but I didn't look away this time. I met him head-on instead of dropping my eyes as I usually did. He kept staring, deep into me. For a brief moment, I wished he would hold me again. Then he turned and made his way to the door, his boots echoing in the empty space. He fingered the cheap dead bolt and the flimsy chain, and looked back at me, still unreadable.

"There's nothing in here worth stealing now, if that's your concern." I tried to make light of everything, just to see if I could get another smile or at least a glimpse of one. He simply stared longer and harder. I squirmed a bit under his unwavering scrutiny. His voice was silent in my head.

"I've been through worse, Mute. I'll survive. It's just stuff."

His eyes were so deep. He tapped the lock, and I heard him loud and clear.

"Lock up behind me."

"I will. Thank you so much, Mute. I really… um… I… just, thank you," I stuttered.

He tapped his watch and pointed at my laptop. *"When is class tomorrow?"*

"I have a class at ten, and need to be at the bar around six.

The city bus stop is pretty close by, so I should be able to get there on time. You don't have to worry about picking me up for work. I have to go to the Lair late tomorrow night after the bar, round eleven, I think. Betsey's watching Blue's kids over at his house, so I'll be working the club bar as well."

He nodded once, turned, and left. I did what he said and locked up the meager protection the cheap brass bar and links offered. Curled up in my bed, I replayed a few of the events of the evening, touching my mouth with my fingertips, before finally falling asleep.

***

Mute left Kat's dismal apartment and waited until he heard her slide the flimsy lock in place. His head and heart were at war, putting him in unfamiliar territory. Not since Maya had he felt anything for a woman other than a need to take one to bed occasionally to scratch an itch. He'd known what Maya was before he gave her his heart and patched her as his. He'd thought they were happy together and it would last a lifetime. He was so in love, her history as a club bunny didn't bother him, and he was even able to overlook her drug history as well. She loved him right back despite his disability, or so he thought. It was supposed to be the perfect life, and was until *that* day happened. The day he came to the clubhouse and found Maya, bare-ass naked, wearing only the property cut he gave her with Joker drilling her from behind.

He had stood in the doorway, silently watching them for several minutes, fingering the small box he had in his pocket and wondering if anyone else knew there was no sound when a heart shattered into a thousand pieces. Joker must've heard something, as he had looked up as he was pumping away at the moaning and writhing Maya, and noticed Mute in the doorway. Instead of being shocked and horrified, he sneered and rammed into Maya harder, stroking his hand over the Property of Mute patch.

It took four brothers to pull him off Joker. Mute barely remembered landing his fist into that grinning face, only seeing red and feeling an overpowering rage at the betrayal of the man who was supposed to be his brother, and the woman who was supposed to be his mate. He was so far in his head, he had heard Brick's voice as if coming from a deep well: rules, Joker being forced into nomad status, and Maya being booted out. He didn't know what had happened to her other than she was completely gone the next day, out of town forever. Mute felt nothing after that. The ring he had carried in his pocket was flung into the river, and along with it the pieces of his dead heart and the vow never to love again.

That was until he came to the bar one night and found Kat.

Mute smoothed a hand over his torso where he still felt the jolt he had experienced earlier tonight. Finding Kat on the roadside shivering in the cold next to her car had done something to him. There had been a pain in his chest that he couldn't explain and didn't understand. His emotions had run the gamut of anger at her for being in that situation even if it wasn't completely her fault, fear for her well-being, and amusement at her actually yelling at him for "yelling" at her. Christ! She'd even made him *laugh*! His gut churned, and he wished he could meet up with her roommate and the nasty-ass boyfriend just once. He got down to his truck, the snow already accumulating on the windshield. He brushed it off, got in, and sat in the driver seat staring at the dancing white flakes. He licked his lips slowly, remembering her sweet taste and fighting the sudden tightening in his jeans.

Fuck me. I shouldn't have kissed her. I don't need another Donna type to deal with.

He knew he was fooling himself. Kat would never be a Donna type. Donna had finally figured out Mute's indifference and had moved on, putting Hammer in her sights. Kat wouldn't have gone after him in the first place, not being the kind to use her body to get what she wanted.

Too soft. Lets everyone walk all over her. Including me.

Mute sat for a moment more and made his decision. Like it or not, Kat was a part of the club. She'd earned her place with her work at the bar, at the Lair, and with the help she gave Betsey and the other members. He would take care of her as he would anyone else in the club. It was his job to protect the club, and since she was a part of it, he would be her protector too, but that was all. Anything else was too much to ask of him—or her.

Problem is, can I protect her from myself, and protect myself from her?

CHAPTER NINE

I came out of my physiology class and found Mute leaning on the wall directly across from the lecture hall. He looked every bit the badass biker, dressed in faded jeans, black boots, and a heavy black leather jacket. He wore his cut over the jacket so everyone could see the patches declaring him to be that badass. His arms were crossed, his face hard and intimidating to anyone looking at him. The silver chain around his neck winked in the fluorescent lights.

"OMG, Katwoman! Is that your boyfriend?" Jessica breathed at me. "He's the one that brought you to the hospital! OMG, he is sooo big!"

I cringed a little at the Katwoman nickname she'd given me the night I showed up at the hospital wearing that costume.

"Not a boyfriend. Coworker, more or less, and he's helping me out since my car died," I said, trying to sound flippant. He had shown up at my place this morning in his truck and driven me to class. He had been back to his surly disagreeable self. The considerate man who held me, laughed out loud, and kissed me so thoroughly was gone. This was not completely unexpected, but still, he did show up unasked to help me. I wasn't really sure what to expect from him at this point, but I thought something had changed between us. "Everything okay, Mute?"

He got off the wall and jerked his head to the outside doors.

Jessica gasped and oohed. I thought she was going to melt into a little puddle or try to climb him like a tree.

We reached his truck, and he opened the passenger door for me to get in. I climbed up, a little bewildered, but I wasn't going to turn down a ride. He got in, closed his door, and turned to me and laid a white box in my lap.

My eyes widened. "Is this for me?"

He scowled and gestured for me to open the box. It was a top-of-the-line smartphone, charged up and ready to go. The number was written on a piece of paper just inside the box.

I gulped. "I… I… I… It's too much, Mute! I don't have money to pay you back."

Mute sighed, pulled out his own phone, and started texting. A moment later, the new phone in my hands beeped.

Mute: Not a big deal. I get two extra lines on my plan. Mackie has one and you got the other.

We were really talking now. Not just words I made up in my head. I was right. Something big had changed between us.

He kept texting.

Mute: Getting your shit together and moving today

"What?"

Mute: I didnt stutter.

He grinned.

I rolled my eyes and watched as his broad fingers flew over the tiny keyboard.

Mute: Your place is shit and too much mony. You cant afford it. Bad locks. Not safe. Moving in with Mackie. He could use the help round the house.

I was stunned to silence. Who was this man? He kept typing.

Mute: Mackies the big gray house half mile from the bar. Upstairs is for rent. His place is the bottom floor. He gets money from the goverment because of his missing arm but what he needs is someone to help him out around the house. He don't get around to good. The Parkinsons dizeaze is getting worse. Rent is cooking some, cleaning up, getting groceries, givng him his pills, that sort of thing.

I relaxed a little. This was the protector side of Mute coming out for Mackie. This had nothing to do with me.

Mute: Mackies got an old Dodge Intrepid. Ugly ass beige thing but it runs good. Your car is dead. Only worth a few parts that might still work. You use Mackies car for a while. He cant drive no more. Parkinson's is getting to bad.

I was overwhelmed. Good luck like this rarely happened to me, but since I'd hooked up with this club, life had gotten better. "I don't know what to say. It's too much."

Mute: You just keep doing what you doing. Your a

part of the club. I protect the club. I protect you. Payback is you take care of Betsey and Mackie.

"Okay. I can do that," I said to him, grinning from ear to ear. Life suddenly looked a little brighter. Perhaps my run of bad luck was over.

Mute: As far as the other, dont make a big deal of it. It happened. Its over. Wont happen again.

Life got a little dimmer. "Um… I guess you mean when you kissed me?"

He all but growled at me and nodded. Yes, that was what he meant. Maybe nothing changed between us after all.

Mute: I said dont make a big deal out of it. This is just me helping you to help Mackie and the club. Nothing more. It wont hapen again.

"I understand," I told him in a small voice. Inside, my heart broke just a little bit. For a brief moment last night, I'd felt special. Like *I* mattered. *Me.* But what really mattered was what I could do for the club. I guess it could be worse. Mute was rough, but he did care about Mackie and the club enough to include me. I could feel good being under that umbrella, as long as I did what he said. No one owed me a life, so it was up to me to make the best of whatever joy I was given.

He drove to my apartment and watched while I gathered and packed the few things that were mine. He made me leave the ratty couch and mattress, saying Mackie had nicer stuff for me to use. His exact words were "Goodwill don't even want your shit."

He drove me to Mackie's house. I was a little surprised to

see how big it was. It was set about five hundred yards back from the road at the end of a long driveway on about an acre of neatly trimmed land. It was an older two-story farmhouse that looked like it had been modified and had some nice add-ons. The gray siding looked recently installed; there was a large front porch and a side deck with a large grill hooked up. There were several outbuildings, including a nicely built garage and workshop, a small greenhouse, a storage shed with a large woodpile stacked at its side, and a mother-in-law cottage way in the back. The massive yard was full of green grass, and the property was surrounded by trees. You could see the main road, but the house would be difficult to spot unless you were looking for it.

Mackie was on the porch and apparently expecting me.

"Welcome home, darling!" he greeted me with his usual enthusiasm. "Ya get the top bunk, I'm taking the bottom. Everything should be ready for ya."

Mute grabbed the two boxes that held my stuff and tromped up the steep, narrow stairs. The wood creaked with every step. There were four big bedrooms up there, two on each side, and a large bathroom at the top of the steps. Two of the rooms were obviously storage, and the other two were furnished as a bedroom and connected sitting room. I entered the sitting room first, as it was the first one on the right. It held a simple futon sofa covered in plain brown, with a Native American print rug in greens, blues, and reds on the wood floor. There was a flat-screen TV set up in one corner, along with a Blu-ray player and some empty shelves. An old-fashioned roll top desk sat in one corner, the top up revealing lots of little cubby holes. A new power strip sat on the top, obviously put there for my laptop.

I followed Mute through the connecting door to the bedroom.

It was beautiful. The bedroom was painted a light slate gray with white trim. The hardwood floors were covered with several thick, shaggy white rugs. The bed was an old-fashioned brass frame with several fluffy pillows, the colorful comforter in stripes of different blues, white, and gray. There was an antique dresser of darker wood, a matching nightstand, and a vanity table. The two rooms were bigger than my apartment. I didn't need to see the bathroom to know it was fabulous as well.

"I can't believe all of this is for me." Tears filled my eyes at the older man's generosity.

Mackie harrumphed from the bottom of the steps.

"I didn't do nothin'. That was Mute going to the Walmart, hauling and settin' up your stuff. I cain't get up them steps no more. The whole second floor is yours."

I turned to Mute in surprise and a little confusion. He had been so adamant about the kiss we shared meaning nothing to him. Maybe just an impulse at the time, since he'd been laughing in that strange grunting noise.

If he kissed me because of the timing, then why do all this for me?

Mute was not happy with Mackie's announcement, and it showed. His face was dark and he looked at me with his angry Hulk look. I could hear his voice in my head warning me.

"Don't start nothing!"

I knew then he was doing this mainly for Mackie's benefit. Mackie would have been the one to go to Walmart and set up these rooms for me had he been able to do so, but his disease was progressing rapidly, and getting around was harder and harder for him. Even though this was not really about me, I still got to reap some wonderful rewards.

I ignored the silent hostile voice and moved in, putting my arms around Mute's body. "I understand, Mute, but thank you for all of this. I'll pay you back as soon as I can."

His jaw clenched and unclenched like he was grinding his teeth. He gave a sharp nod and pushed past me to tromp down the steps, his heavy tread echoing throughout the house. The screen door slapped against the frame. A moment later, I heard the growl of his truck as he took off.

A text message beeped on my phone.

Mute: No payback for gifts. Just do your job and take care of Mackie.

"Rude-ass bastard!" Mackie commented. "Whelp, his loss is my gain! You got KP duty tonight, darlin'. What's fer supper?"

I laughed and went downstairs into the modern kitchen to scrounge up something to feed my friend and new roomie.

CHAPTER TEN

A loud thwack sounded outside, and I looked through the kitchen window above the sink. Mute was chopping wood, his bare back to me and steam rising from his body in the cold winter air. His hair was gathered back in a short ponytail at the base of his neck, and I could clearly see his club tattoo. A colorful green, gold, and black dragon, wings spanning his broad shoulders, long talons tipped in red, and breathing fire. It was a beautiful work of art, one of several. He had other colorful tattoos on his chest and arms.

All three of us were living together, so to speak, and had settled into a routine. Mute was renting the one-bedroom mother-in-law cottage toward the back of the property. His rent was keeping the yard and landscaping up, house repairs as needed, and keeping the wood stacked up for the fireplace and woodstove. Mackie spent his days puttering around his greenhouse, or watching TV in his big reclining chair. I went to classes, worked at the bar, cleaned for Mackie, and cooked for all three of us. It became routine for Mute to walk in the house about the time I set dinner on the table. The first night, when I put a whole roasted chicken, fresh green beans, mashed potatoes and gravy, and homemade biscuits on the table, Mackie was beside himself and texted Mute, insisting that he come join us. Both men had gorged themselves silly, and Mackie had been in rare form.

"Oh, darlin', I think I just died and gone to heaven! Them biscuits is the best I ever ate! You should be on one of them fancy cooking shows, you know, like them ones that has prize money at the end. Whadya think, Mute? Ain't she somethin'?"

Mute just looked at him with one eyebrow cocked and picked up another biscuit. I think he consumed about half the chicken by himself, along with a generous amount of the beans and potatoes. I had hoped to get a few days' worth of leftovers, but I kissed that thought goodbye when I saw Mute take seconds and then thirds. It was nice seeing both men enjoy their food.

Mackie continued to rave about my cooking, until I got red in the face from embarrassment.

"Who taught you how to cook so good? Your mama?"

I stiffened a bit, but answered with a smile. I felt comfortable in this place with Mackie, and thought it was a safe place for me. Not sure why I did it, but I decided to open up a bit about my life.

"No. I don't know who my real parents are. Never met them. I was left as a baby at the hospital. I bounced around lots of homes for a while, but when I started school, I had one foster home I got to stay in for about six years. That was

with Millie. She was more like a grandmother than a mom, but she taught me a lot about cooking, housekeeping, and just taking care of people. She was a retired nurse and a wonderful, giving person. I was twelve when the social workers decided she was too old to take care of me anymore and moved me somewhere else. I heard she passed away before I graduated high school. I think she's the reason I decided to go into nursing. She was the best home I've ever had."

I paused for a minute, and then grinned at Mackie's serious face. "Not counting this one, of course!"

He guffawed loudly and slapped his thigh.

"Hot damn, girl! You a good 'un! Ain't that right, Mute?"

Mute had just looked up from spreading butter over the steaming white bread. His eyes were on mine, but he wasn't scowling for a change. There had been a look of understanding or even comradery on his face.

I shook myself from the memory, lifted my phone, and tapped out a message to him.

Me: I'm not cooking tonight because of the Christmas party. I can make you a light snack if you need something. I told Betsey I'd be at the Lair at 6:00 to help her set up. Does that work for you?

I watched as Mute put down the ax and checked his phone. He turned to the window, wiping the sweat from his brow, and gave me a nod and a thumbs-up.

Mute had changed a lot toward me since the night my Fred passed on to wherever cars go, and my subsequent move into Mackie's and his domain. I would get random texts from him asking if I needed anything from the grocery store he could pick up, what was I cooking tonight, what time my classes were over, and what time I was working. If he was around when I got home from the store, he would unload the bags of food for me. He started driving us both to work at the bar, and Mackie would ride with us on the nights he was up for getting out of the house and being around people. Those nights that Mackie just couldn't do much, Mute would leave the bar several times during the shift to check on him, and then come back to get me when the bar closed. Mute always came home now, abandoning his room at the Lair. He ate most of his meals with us, and spent time with Mackie in front of the TV. True to his word, he never kissed me again, never even touched me, but he was as solicitous of me as anyone had ever been.

Mackie had good days and bad days. His medications sometimes worked and sometimes left him like a zombie. I could see the old man going downhill, but there wasn't much Mute or I could do about it. He was planning on coming to the Christmas party, but he may or may not feel up to staying long. Mute and I had decided we would drive both the car and the truck. That way one of us could bring Mackie home when he needed to go.

The Lair was lit up with hundreds of colored Christmas lights. Betsey had told me that Brick was the one responsible. He loved putting up lights, decorating the giant Christmas tree, and all things that had to do with the holiday. He played Santa every year for the kids, cramming himself into a red suit and gluing on a fake beard. I had never had the childhood Christmas of believing in Santa and getting lots of presents under the tree. Millie had come close with a little artificial tree and homemade decorations, but it wasn't that big of an event. I couldn't help but get into the holiday this time, as Brick and Betsey's enthusiasm bled over into every business the club owned.

The Lair became crowded quickly with all the families and kids. There were just as many lights on the inside of the lodge as the outside, blinking in tandem. Christmas music was playing from the giant speakers. Even the deer head that normally sported a baseball cap was decked out in a Santa hat, beard, and red bulb on his nose. The fresh scent of the ten-foot tinsel-covered pine tree mixed with the mouthwatering aromas of roasted turkey and ham. There were also several platters of deer meat, and a roast duck. Just like the barbecue at Halloween, the club provided meats, and the rest was potluck. I'd baked three cakes from recipes I learned from Millie so many years ago, five-flavor pound cake, butternut vanilla cake, and super chocolate fudge cake. I added them to the groaning table of food. Betsey directed the kitchen, and walked around always being a great hostess. People milled about laughing, drinking, and eating. Kids ran around chasing each other. Men played pool or darts, and the beer flowed freely.

I stayed behind the bar for the most part, serving beer and mixing drinks. I was more comfortable working than not, and the bar helped me to hide. It also helped to keep an eye on Mackie. He was over on one of the couches, telling a group of kids some of his war stories. I could tell he was getting tired, but he was having too good a time to leave.

"BOOM!" he yelled, bugging his eyes out and flinging his hand in the air. "Smoke was everywhere! People screaming and cussing, running around worse than chickens with their heads cut off!"

Mute came behind the bar carrying another beer keg. He tapped it and switched it out with the empty one.

"Thanks, Mute. I'm going to make an empties round while you're here."

He rolled his eyes and quirked an eyebrow.

"Not at work tonight," I heard in my head. It was getting easier and easier to read his thoughts, and I was getting more and more comfortable doing it. Mute wasn't nearly as scary to me as he once was, and although he did his best to remain gruff and aloof, living around him had shown me his true colors.

I grinned at him as I lifted the bar bridge. "I know, I know, but a little effort will make less work tomorrow when we have to come clean up this mess."

I took Mackie a fresh beer to check on him, and gathered up a handful of empty bottles and Solo cups to toss in the rapidly filling trash cans. I spotted Stud on one of the corner couches, watching several of the brothers playing an Xbox racing game. He still had a soft cast on his arm, but his ankle was healed enough that he was off the crutches. Nikki was snuggled up against him wearing a short green elf dress and candy-cane-striped stockings. She was stroking his chest, and his good arm was around her. I felt a twinge of regret, wondering if that could've been me there curled up into his

129

strong body.

"Past is past," Mackie had intoned at me more than once over morning coffee conversations when it was just us at the kitchen table. "No use doin' woulda-coulda-shoulda in this life, darlin'. Gotta keep moving forward."

"Ho, Ho, Ho! Merry Christmas!!" Brick's Santa appearance was heralded by the screams of excited young children. They surrounded the red-suited man wearing a Dragon Runner's cut with cries of "Santa! Santa!" The older ones followed more slowly, but with the same enthusiasm.

"Who's been naughty this year, and who's been nice?" Several of the prospects came in carrying huge boxes filled with red, white, and green Christmas stockings.

"I've been good, Santa!"

"Me too!"

"I haven't been bad at all!"

"Mama says I'm good *all* the time!"

Brick/Santa played the game a few more minutes, whipping the kids into a frenzy.

"Well I guess everyone has been good enough for this year. Let's see what Santa has in his pack, hmm?"

Each kid had a stocking with his or her name on it. The choruses of "I'm good" changed to "Look what I got!" as they pulled out dolls, cars, Play-Doh, Lego, and other bits.

"Brick loves this shit, cain't you tell?" Betsey sat down at the bar while I scurried back behind it again. I put together a margarita on the rocks for her, no salt, as was her preference.

"Yes, I can tell he does. It's wonderful that you and he

do so much for the club. The kids are having a blast. So's Mackie." I nodded toward the old man.

She took a sip of the drink and sighed.

"Oh, that's good!" She set down the glass and tapped the rim with a bright red fingernail before grabbing my hand and holding it tight. "Finals all done with?"

"Yes, and I managed to get all A's this time."

"Good for you, girl. Nice not to have that stress. Ain't been a bad year for anyone. The businesses are all in the black. A few problems been cropping up with the books and inventories, but so far nothing too big. Stud keeps that mess under control, thank the Lord! It would drive me batshit crazy to deal with all that!"

She paused long enough to take another sip of her drink and reload for the next round of words.

"Brick, I mean Santa, will get to the smaller stockings in a bit for the adults. Those have bonuses for the boys. Earned for their work and their loyalty to the club and to each other. This is a big deal for Brick, as well as the club. You know we've had a rough history, and this is a way of reminding us that we went through some tough times but came out on top. We're stronger as a family, and we wanna keep it that way."

Indeed, Brick was handing out smaller stockings to the club members, hugging each one and delivering a single slap on the back of their cut.

Betsey grinned, set her drink on the bar, and clapped her hands together.

"This is my favorite part! These next stockings are the Secret Santa ones. We get to pick a club person to buy for and go a little crazy. Everyone gets something good."

I looked up in horror. "Oh shit, Betsey! I didn't know! I didn't get anything for anyone!"

She flipped her hand up and let out a pshhhhht!

"Ain't no problem, darlin'. You're givin' enough by takin' care of Mackie. Next year, however, is a different story. I'll send you a list a'what I want." She smiled and gave me a friendly tap on the shoulder.

The old ladies got stockings handed to them filled with jewelry, gift certificates, purses, and other stuff. Mackie was grinning from ear to ear with his collection of heirloom vegetable seeds. Even Nikki and Donna got stockings.

"Here, Kat, this one's for you from me an' Betsey, but this didn't fit in it."

My eyes got wide as Brick handed me a waist-length black leather jacket with long fringe hanging from the arms and across the back and front.

"Mute let us know what happened to your stuff. Thought this might come in handy." The fake white beard spoke solemnly and kindly to me.

My eyes grew moist. "I... I... don't know what to say!"

"Pssht! Say 'thank you, Brick' and try it on! Came from our leather shop. Mute ordered it special." Betsey's eyes were a little moist as well.

The jacket was beautifully made. The smell of the buttery leather tickled my nose as I slipped it over my shoulders. The cut and fit were perfect, and I could feel its heavy warmth settle over me like a deep hug.

"It's wonderful," I breathed, brushing the fringe hanging

from the front with my fingertips. "I've never had anything like it before."

"Darlin', that ain't all! Open the rest of your secret Santa stocking."

I brushed at my eyes to hide their watering, and did as Betsey bid. Inside the stocking were a handful of store gift certificates: Macy's, Kohl's, Harley-Davidson store, and Victoria's Secret. Each one in the amount of five hundred dollars.

"Wooo! You done good, Mute!" Molly wandered over and clapped her hands together. "We're going shoppin', girlfriend! I can hear those after-Christmas sales calling our names!"

Mute? Mute gave me two thousand dollars' worth of clothing store gift certificates. I turned to him, my mouth hanging open in amazement. Mute was my secret Santa? He was holding his phone and texting. My phone beeped, and I glanced at his message.

Mute: I dont shop much. best I coud think of. Merry Christmas, Kat.

I shook my head, completely overwhelmed. "I... I... j-just can't believe you did all this for m-me! You didn't really like me much, but the last f-f-few weeks—"

"Merry fuckin' Christmas, y'all!" a loud, rude voice interrupted.

My stomach clenched. Joker was back. He came in the front door with Box, carrying a large knapsack and wearing a weird contraption on his head. An elastic band was strapped around a Christmas baseball cap. It was holding a flexible stick resembling a small fishing pole that bobbed up and down with a sprig of mistletoe on the end.

Betsey harrumphed and shook a finger at him. "You'd best not be here to make trouble, Joker! Brick's forgiven you for the last time, but you start disrespecting again—"

"Betsey, my one and only love! Please tell me you'll run away with me tonight! Kiss me, darling," he sang to her. "Lookie! I brought my own mistletoe!" He bobbled his head and the sprig moved up and down.

She laughed as his lips smacked loudly on her cheek.

"No problems, Joker! I mean it!" She shook a finger at him again as he bounced over to Molly, who pushed him away.

"Ugh! Get away from me with that stuff!"

"Aw! Molly, my precious!" he crooned.

"I thought I was your favorite!" Betsey teased.

"There's plenty of the Joker to go around, ladies!" He spread his arms wide, the picture of a fun-loving guy.

Most of the other people were laughing at his antics. A few were eyeing him with mistrust. Stud was looking daggers at him from his place on the couch. Mackie was shaking his head. I turned to see Mute had moved to just behind me.

Mute was barely containing his fury, his hands clenching and unclenching, his jaw set in a hard line. Joker bounced over to us, grinning widely.

"I'm here to make amends for my behavior the last time we spoke, dearest Pussy Kat. Please accept my humblest apologies!" He made an elegant courtier's bow, the sprig of mistletoe bobbing around freely.

"Um… apology accepted," I stammered, unable to think of anything else to say. I felt Mute's arm around me, pulling me to the side and shuffling me behind him, putting himself between Joker and me.

"Ho, ho, ho! What is this? Beauty and the beast, eh? Never fear, dearest Pussy Kat! I'll fight anyone who calls you a beast!" Joker declared, dancing away.

I took a chance and placed my hand lightly on Mute's arm. He always wore a black Henley under his cut, and I could feel the tightness of his muscles under the soft cloth. "It's okay, Mute. He won't make trouble. Too many people around."

Mute didn't take his eyes off Joker as he flitted around the room. His arm moved, draping around my shoulders and pulling me close to his side. The feeling of protection and security bloomed warm in my gut as I felt the heat from his body surround me. He had my back. He had me.

I couldn't help myself. I was under his heavy arm, curling into his body, so it was natural that I put my arms around him, holding him close and laying my head against his shoulder.

"Thank you for everything, Mute. I don't have the words to tell you how grateful I am for everything you've done for me."

His glittering eyes left Joker and came to mine. He looked at me with a depth I hadn't seen in him before, and my breath left me. Someday, I would look back and know this was the turning point. This was when I, Katrina Vega, was silently claimed by a Dragon Runner called Mute. I became his woman, his old lady then and there, just like a puzzle piece fitting into another one, perfectly locked into place. This was my place, and it made me feel complete. His eyes dropped to my mouth, and he raised a hand to stroke a gentle finger over my lower lip. I felt the bottom drop out of my stomach in anticipation as he swayed forward to take what now belonged to him.

A loud explosion suddenly rocked the room, and the walls shook violently. The deer head with the Santa hat and Rudolph nose fell off the wall. Women screamed and ducked, covering their heads. Some ran outside in confusion. Betsey looked out the window.

"Brick! The bar is on fire!" she screamed, pointing at the visible orange flames at the bottom of the hill.

Brick's authoritative voice boomed out, the jolly Santa gone.

"Lock down! You know the drill! Dragon Runners to me! Let's go!"

Mute dropped his arm from me and pointed to Betsey and Mackie.

"Take your cues from Betsey. Lock everything down. Take care of Mackie. I'll be back when I can. Do not leave."

I started to protest. "But Mackie's pills! What if something happens?"

He grabbed my face and stared into my eyes, not in anger, but with a seriousness I had never seen before. His mouth slammed down on mine, kissing me deep and hard. It ended just as quickly as it started.

"Stay here, stay safe. Promise me!" his intense look conveyed.

"I'll take care of business here," I said, more calmly than I felt. I was stunned from the kiss and the sudden change in our relationship. "Please be careful!"

He left with the other bikers. Stud remained, but since there wasn't much he could do with one arm, he limped back and forth in front of the bay windows, looking down at the burning building.

"Goddammit! Motherfuckers!" he cursed, more harshly than I had ever heard him.

Betsey rallied herself and the other women. "Right, then. Ladies, if you have a cabin already reserved, get yourselves there and your kids to bed. Locks and alarms. Gate's already closed to the compound, so we're solid, but if you don't feel safe in your own places, go get your stuff and spread out in here or the loft upstairs. Nikki, Donna, and you others, get started cleaning up, and don't make me come after your asses! Just put the trash outside the back door. Molly and Tambre, you sort the rest of the leftover cabins and any spare rooms we have here. Bedding, towels, toiletries, other supplies. Gonna be a full house tonight. Kat, you check the condition of the kitchen, and start packing away the food. See what else we have in the pantry and see how much booze we got. The boys are gonna want it later. I'll join you as soon as I get my grandkids settled upstairs. Don't know how long this lockdown is going to last, but we need to be prepared for whatever."

"What can I do to help?" Mackie asked, still seated on

a couch.

Betsey handed him a pair of binoculars and her phone.

"Watch what you can and listen for my phone. Brick will call me with whatever he finds at some point, but right now I need to keep busy. Come on, Cody an' Shells, let's get you up to bed."

Betsey took the two softly crying and confused children upstairs. Mackie took his position to the side of the window, the binoculars glued to his eyes. Stud stood awkwardly by him, still muttering and cursing as he too watched the fire in the distance. Donna and Nikki apparently took Betsey seriously. They and the other women were clearing empties, wiping tables, and taking out the trash. I left and went into the kitchen. Betsey wasn't the only one who needed to be busy.

Hours later, the kids were in bed, the food put away, and the kitchen nearly finished. My mind started to wander as I was mopping the floor.

Mute kissed me again, I thought as I stored leftovers, put dishes in the big industrial dishwasher, and wiped counters. *He said he wouldn't do it again, but he did. He gave me money for clothes. A lot of it. He's cursed at me. He got me a place to live. He gets mad at me for no reason. He protected me. He fucked another woman right in front of me, maybe deliberately. He stood between me and someone who might've hurt me. He got me a phone when I needed one and couldn't afford it. He hates me. He wants me. He loves me.*

I stopped moving around. *No.* I shook my head. *Don't go*

there, Kat. Not the time.

Tambre came into the kitchen with an armful of dishes. She took one look at my face and dumped the whole pile in the sink. She was a little taller than me, mainly because she liked to wear heels with everything. She was a beautiful woman, both inside and out. She hugged me close and I felt her quiet strength seep into me, holding me up.

"He's a hard man. Been through more in his lifetime than most of the others in the club, and it wasn't pretty. Seen more. Done more. His hands have been dirty, and will be dirty again. I've watched it happen since he was a kid and Brick found him scroungin' for food outta the bar dumpster. The stuff he lived with, the stuff he lived through, can leave scars on people. I 'spect you know that, since you weren't brought up with silver spoons or roses either."

She moved away and started unloading the dishwasher, still steaming from its four-minute cycle. I picked up the stacked dishes and put them away.

"We been talking, me and Betsey and Molly. 'Bout you and the club. You ain't an old lady—" She paused and looked at me with her wise eyes, and added, "—yet." She shifted more dishes to the counter.

"You ain't a bunny neither, and ain't gonna be, but you still got a place here. Your own place. Makes you family no matter what. Molly really wants you with Stud. I know that boy was interested, but not enough, not like Mute. When Stud looks at you, I see a man who likes you and wants you."

She stopped and took both my hands in hers. "When Mute looks at you, I see a man who *needs* you and needs you bad. Needs you so bad it consumes him every day. I see him fight it like he has everything else in his life. He's trying to not have that need, but it's there and he's losing and he's scared. Scared bad. Both of you got walls, thick and tall ones. You been looking at each other over them walls for a long time now, and they're cracking. One of you had to take the risk in breaking them down, and it *is a risk*. A scary one, 'cause both y'alls hearts is involved and y'all have been bruised up a time or two in the past. You got to decide if he's worth that risk."

Molly appeared in the doorway, her face unusually solemn.

"Boys are back."

CHAPTER ELEVEN

The men who returned were milling around the room, too restless to sit. The club women were filling their support roles. Betsey had pulled some beers from the cooler. Tambre carried one to Taz and hugged him close, giving him the strength she gave me. Mute wasn't with them.

Brick looked his age, like the world rested on his shoulders, and in a way, it did.

"Bar is gone, a total loss. Didn't get the boat house or the dock. Fire chief has to do a deeper investigation, but thinks it was a gas leak that did it. There's evidence that says it was deliberate, but he's got to confirm that. Arson is a hard one to prove, but Bill says whoever set it didn't hide nothing."

There was a collective gasp around the room. The men's faces looked even grimmer. I glanced at Betsey to see how she was taking the news. Tears flowed down her face, and she hurried to Brick's side. She took his hand and stood by him, every bit the club queen, even though her world had just crumbled to ash.

"Good news is no one got hurt. Everyone stays here for the rest of the night. Gates are locked and alarms are set. Get some sleep. Church in the morning. Nine o'clock sharp."

He didn't bother with saying Merry Christmas as he and Betsey quietly went up the stairs and into their suite.

Men and women wandered off to their places, some to the cabins and some to rooms. I found out Mackie was given one of the lower club rooms for the night and had already gone to bed. Tambre and Taz left for their private cabin, as did Molly and Cutter. Stud retired to his room, taking Nikki with him.

I wasn't sure what I was supposed to do. The front door behind me opened up. Mute was there with three backpacks over his massive shoulders, and a handful of plastic grocery bags. He had made a run back to Mackie's house. He quirked an eyebrow at me.

"Where's Mackie?"

"Molly got him set up in room four downstairs. He may be asleep by now, but really needs to take his pills."

Mute jerked his head in a nod, and went to take a pack to Mackie, and wake him up if needed. I put the groceries he'd brought away, and wiped the counters one more time. He was standing in the middle of the great room when I came back. He stood in front of me, his strong arms at his sides, looking at me. I recognized those walls Tambre was talking about, but she was wrong. Those walls weren't cracking. Those walls were crumbled into dust. Mute was raw, uncovered, and unguarded. He was hiding nothing, and was more vulnerable than I'd thought he could ever be. I could see it. I could feel it. I knew what he was asking, but his voice was silent in my head. It was my turn.

I took three bounding steps and launched myself at him, my legs and arms going around him as far as they could, trusting he was going to catch me. Trusting him with everything. He caught me, wrapping me tight, holding me close, burying his face in my neck, breathing me in. I held on for dear life. Whatever happened tomorrow, if this was just a fluke, a one-time thing, I didn't care. I just wanted tonight.

He carried me to his room in the back of the lodge. It was one of the larger ones, with a private bathroom and small sitting area. The bed was covered in a thin-striped blue, black, and tan comforter. A small nightstand was next to it, with a single drawer and small lamp made from a short log. A small flat-screen TV was on the wall in front of a large oversized recliner in one corner, and another chair held an assortment of clothes, both draped and folded. There was a large American flag pinned to the wall behind the bed, and a couple of motorcycle posters on the other walls. It wasn't completely sparse, but everything in the room screamed, "Single male biker."

He set me on my feet next to the bed, relaxing his grip on me, but didn't let go. I looked into the dark depths of his eyes, and for the first time ever saw uncertainty. He stroked my cheek softly with the tips of his fingers, and ran his thumb over my lips. I could feel and hear him asking, *"Do you really want this? Do you want me?"*

In all the months I'd been around him, I'd never seen

Mute so defenseless. I had the power to break him if I rejected him at his moment.

"What is your real name?" I asked against his thumb. He paused, then reached for his phone. I put my hand over his in a bold move to stop him.

"No," I said firmly "Don't text me." I took a breath and pierced his eyes with mine. "Tell me."

He stared, eyes glazing over, his lips parted. He took several deep breaths. I couldn't tell whether I'd just pissed him off, made him laugh, or something else.

"Alec," he managed to say on a harsh growling whisper. It was barely audible, but it was there.

I ran my hands over his hard chest and up to his face, tangling in the chains around his neck, and burying them in his thick hair at the back of his neck. I could feel him trembling, as if he was scared of me.

"Make love to me, Alec. Please."

He kissed me slow, savoring, totally in contrast with his rough and tough badass biker image. For such a hard man, his lips were incredibly soft as they gently sucked at mine. The tip of his tongue ran over my bottom lip, and I opened my mouth, both in shock and invitation. He took it and swept inside. He slanted his mouth against mine and pulled me closer, delving and exploring deeper. Electricity zapped through me, and my sex clenched in response. I could feel myself growing wet. My breasts swelled, and my nipples hardened and pulsed. Mute nipped at my lips, pulling the lower one between his teeth to suck at it and stroke it softly with his tongue. He repeated it with my upper lip, and then delved in again, tasting me deeply. I played with him, touching his tongue with mine, stroking boldly. He moved one arm lower, over my bottom, and pressed me into his body. I could feel his hard arousal just above my pelvis. I felt out of control. I was one big ball of need. I'd never been that way before and it terrified me, but I wanted this more than anything, and I reveled in the sensation.

Mute must have felt the change in me. He drew back, ending the devastating kiss, hovering over my mouth so we shared breaths for a moment or two. I was shaking, my legs like jelly. He pulled back just enough to pull my T-shirt over my head, my plain bra following. He whipped off his own shirt, and pulled me back into his body, crushing my breasts into his warm chest as if he couldn't bear to be separated. He kissed me again. Long. Slow. Deep.

I was burning up by the time we were both naked and on the bed. He laid me there with my back on the comforter, and he curled in to my side. His touches were reverent, treating me like the greatest gift he had ever been given. He loved my body with his eyes, his fingers, his mouth and tongue, tasting me and savoring every bite. He lingered over my breasts, his tongue both rough and soft, and I arched my back, moaning at the electricity that zapped through me. His fingers trailed over every inch of my body, exploring every curve, every crevice.

Claiming me.

He worshipped me with his mouth, sucking and licking at me in an experience I'd never had, driving me higher and higher. I clutched at his head, crying out as the orgasm hit me. It was the first real one I'd ever felt and the power in it was overwhelming. I heard the soft crinkle of plastic as he opened a condom wrapper with his teeth. He sheathed himself and moved over me, covering me with his heat, his hips settling between my legs and his forearms on either side of my shoulders. He gazed into my eyes as his hard tip touched my wetness and I gasped when he pressed forward, breaching my opening. He was big, and his unyielding push stretched me to the point of pain.

He paused when he was all the way inside, giving me a moment to get used to him being there. I looked back at him, my hands on his strong shoulders, holding him to me. His dark eyes were usually unreadable or irritable but now, as his body was joined with mine, I was shocked at the depth of emotion in them. I never knew I was empty until he filled me with himself.

I struggled for breath, unable to look away when he began to move, sliding almost all the way out and then pressing back in. I lifted my hips in time with him, taking him in deeper, longer, writhing under him as he relentlessly drove me higher. It stunned me to hear the noises I was making as his thrusts grew faster and more determined, drawing out every bit of pleasure there was. He watched me when I climaxed again. It was harder, stronger, and so powerful I couldn't look away. I cried his real name as my body came apart under him. He closed his eyes and dropped his mouth on mine, his tongue still vaguely tasting of me. He kissed me with an intensity I knew was for me and only me. His body grew rigid as he drove into me a few more times and fiercely came.

Heat poured off his body, and sweat covered both of us. He didn't move for several minutes, still rock-hard inside me. He finally lifted his head from my neck and stroked my hair, his eyes roaming my face. I was shocked to see them wet. Several tears made their way down his cheeks. This silent rock of a man had given something to me. Something big. He was completely open, exposed, and unprotected. He was mine. I raised my head and kissed him, tracing my tongue over his lips. He kissed me back, opening his mouth and letting me inside.

He withdrew from me and left the bed, his bare feet slipping along the thin green carpet. He disposed of the condom and came back to me, curling up behind me, tucking me in close and wrapping a heavy arm over my middle. Since neither of us bothered to put on any clothes, we were touching skin to skin at maximum contact. I lay there, unashamed and not embarrassed at all. I hid nothing from him as I touched his arm, running my fingers over his ink.

The few times I'd slept with the one boyfriend I had in the past always felt like an obligation rather than an act of love. When he wanted sex, I was a convenient place to put his dick. That was it. That was the sum total of my sex life. I never got into masturbating much, just feeling it was more trouble than it was worth.

The orgasms Mute had just given me destroyed my previous thoughts about sex. I'd never thought I would have this deep connection with anyone. I didn't think it was even possible to have it. I'd heard of people saying they'd found their soul mate, but I didn't think it was real. Now, with Mute lying behind me, his fingers moving in random patterns over my skin, I could admit that perhaps it was real. I put my hand over his and felt his breath against the behind my ear as he pressed those beautiful lips against my flesh. Was this real? Was this for me? Might I dare hope for more? The warmth of his body and his gentle touches was lulling me off to sleep. I could feel my eyelids growing heavier as I drifted. Even if this wasn't real, I at least had tonight, and I was going to keep it. At least for the moment, I was totally and completely loved.

***

Mute woke with the rising sun barely coming over the horizon. Pale strips of light came through the blinds of his room, decorating the bed. He was on his back, Kat's nude body curled into him, his arm around her holding her close. He gazed for a moment at her still form, then shifted and pressed his lips against her forehead. Easing away from her, he left the bed and went into the bathroom and showered off the long night of sex with his woman. He didn't want to lose the smell of her from his body, but he also didn't want to share it. She was his and his alone.

He put on his cut, grabbed his cigarettes from the messy dresser top and headed outside into the crisp cold air. Mute tapped out a white stick, looked at it, and put it back in the pack. There was enough ashy smell from the burnt building without him adding to it. His mouth quirked, thinking that it wouldn't be long before Kat gave him shit about the habit.

Kat. My old lady. He thought as he watched the world wake up to a new day. *Gotta get her a patch. My patch.* The one he had for Maya had been destroyed years ago and even if he still had it, he would never disrespect Kat by putting another woman's patch on her.

Fuck, how did this happen? Mute thought to himself. He thought he had loved Maya, and after her betrayal, he had vowed not to fall into that trap again. Kat had avoided him like crazy, and he had done everything he could to push her away. Somehow, she still ended up burrowing her way into his thoughts and his life until he couldn't imagine having one without her in it. His eyes stared off to the distant mountain range as he relived the past night. He recalled each sigh, every touch, the taste of her mouth, and the feel of her pussy as she welcomed him home. All of it had filled his heart to bursting with such emotion, it had leaked from his eyes. No, he couldn't have loved Maya, because he never felt this much for anyone until Kat. This raw unfiltered feeling was new to him, and he was both exhilarated and scared shitless. But he wasn't going to let it go.

Mute's trance was broken by the outside door closing. He turned to see another Dragon Runner, Table, walk out on the deck with a cup of steaming coffee. He nodded a greeting and took a sip of the brew as Mute went back inside. Several other people were up and moving around. Mute ignored them for the most part as he went back to his room and the precious sleeping figure in his bed. He scratched a quick note to her saying he was at church, placing it near her head on the pillow.

Church was held in the conference room on the second floor of the lodge. It held a long, polished cherrywood table and a dozen padded conference chairs. The Dragon Runners' emblem graced the wall behind the head of the table, a dragon skeleton with a long twisting tail, its skull breathing fire. Brick was already up and had made coffee. The other brothers came in one by one, getting cups and settling down. Their expressions were grim.

Brick sat heavily in his seat.

"The fire report is not officially in yet, but the chief still says there's evidence it was arson. Damn bastard didn't hide the gas cans he used. Main gas line was cut and pulled out to sit in the middle of the floor, and a fuckin' burn line led to it. Bill checked it again this mornin' in the daylight and said it's too obvious to be anything else. Bar is a total loss. Stud, how does this balance out with the other businesses and cash flow?"

Stud leaned back in his swivel chair, tapping through accounts on his laptop. "Garage has had some problems with missing inventory, and the books have been off. I can't put my finger on it, but the bank accounts are accurate. Campgrounds are shut down for the winter, minimal use this time of year anyway. We'll see more activity toward Valentine's Day, but only the cabins will be open with any significance. The bar's insurance is up-to-date, and the land we already own outright. We can rebuild if the club decides to do it, maybe even expand a bit. It will take time, and I don't know much about construction, but now is probably not the right time of the year to start it."

Brick sighed and looked around the table.

"Stealin' from the garage. Campground torn up. And now the bar. Seems to me someone is trying to hurt this club. I'm gettin' a mite tired of it. Question is who, why, and what we gonna do about it. Mute, what do we know?"

Mute reached for his own laptop and began rapidly typing. Taz read off the words as Mute's fingers flew over the keyboard.

"Sheriff says a lot of crank has been running in the town. Couple guys in a dark blue tricked-out Monte Carlo have been seen dealin', but so far no one has caught them. Blue said rumor is one guy has a cut with a grim reaper and a devil animal head type emblem, but that's not confirmed. Closest match it could be is the Dead Horsemen over on the Tennessee side."

Taz paused and looked around the table. "I remember them bastards. They used to run guns and drugs with us back in the '80s and '90s. Didn't like it much when we switched over legit. They kept up the shit stuff, but kept it out of our town so far. Bad business back then. We all know the history."

Brick's face went grim when he heard the rival club's name. "We've dealt with those shitheads before when they tried to take over the Tail. They got a lot of young recruits with more partying than brotherhood on their brains. Got balls the size of boulders if they think they can take this club down, but I ain't gonna start no war unless we know for sure they're the ones causing trouble. Their emblem ain't a reaper or devil, but I wouldn't put it past 'em to use someone else's. Them younguns ain't got no respect for nothin'."

He looked around the table at the members present.

"We figure out who's doing this and we finish this bullshit once and for all, but we do it smart. Stud, you get cracking on your magic and shore up the accounts. We're gonna need some extra cash in the immediate future. Taz, you get with the fire chief and get us some firm answers. Mute, you check on hardware and supplies. Cutter, get the garage sorted, but keep it under wraps for now. Business as usual, but it's gonna get real and do it soon. In the meantime, watch your backs, boys. Keep your women and kids safe. Escorts everywhere. You can't be home at night, bring 'em here. Betsey'll get 'em sorted out. Lockdown over for now but we'll bar the door to anyone but club family. This place is a fucking fortress so don't take chances if you feel they should be here. Need a vote, or is everyone good?"

A chorus of "yeahs" sounded around the table. Brick banged the polished wood gavel on a matching disk. The club members got up to leave.

"A word, Mute?" Brick asked.

Mute looked at him and braced, already knowing what the conversation would be about.

"Saw you hooked up last night with Kat. I don't normally get into another brother's business, and I ain't gonna do it now, but I need to know for Betsey, you making a claim?"

Mute stared into his president and mentor's eyes, and moved his head up and down once.

Brick grinned. "Does she know yet?"

Mute's head moved side to side.

Brick's mouth split into a wide grin and he guffawed. "Think you can convince her?"

This time Mute gave one of his rare smiles.

Brick clapped him on the back and roared with laughter. "That's my boy!"

CHAPTER TWELVE

I woke up slowly, stretching like a cat. I had to giggle a bit at the analogy. Late morning sunlight streamed in stripes across the wrecked bed. I sat up, feeling sore in places I normally didn't feel or think about at all. Mute had reached for me several times in the night, making love to me tenderly each time, bringing me to a fulfillment I'd never experienced before. Just recalling the way he touched me, as if I was a treasure he'd found, brought a warm glow to my middle. I read the note he left me about him attending the biker church meeting. I knew it was a serious meeting, and the club would need as much support as it could get.

I went into the bathroom to do my business and take a shower. There was only one towel, slightly damp from Mute's shower earlier. The soap and shampoo was also his and smelled very masculine. I inhaled the scent, and couldn't help but break out in a goofy grin, like a teenager experiencing her first crush. He had brought along a couple of extra changes of clothing, and some of my personal toiletries, so I had my own shampoo, body wash, and toothbrush.

I got under the warm spray, just letting it run over my head and face while I leaned against the cream-colored tiles. My thoughts were a jumbled mess. Part of me was thrilled, influenced by the rose-colored glasses of new romance. The dream of husband, kids, and a white picket fence around a cozy house was something I'd thought I would never have, and in truth, wasn't exactly the future I could envision with a biker. But the reality was, this club was a family, solid and loyal to each other, something else I'd thought I would never have, but was more real to me than the Hollywood version of a happy family. Someone would always have my back. I wanted it. I wanted it bad.

Part of me was scared to death that this was all a dream, an illusion that I would never really fit into, one that would disappear as soon as Mute decided he wasn't interested anymore. I didn't know what to expect, and the uncertainty was killing me. I couldn't be invisible anymore. Mute took care of that last night. People knew my name. I'd made friends, good ones. If this was all going away, would I be able to handle going back to being invisible again?

I heard a click and glanced behind me. Church was over. Mute had entered the bathroom and was in the process of stripping off his clothes. My mouth went dry, and I turned around to face him. I didn't think I could ever get tired of looking at his body. His chest was wide and strong, and he had perfectly delineated abs. Strong arms, strong legs, strong man. His colorful tats stood out on his arms, shoulders, and chest. No piercings, other than his ear. I stared at the juncture of his thighs, where his penis jutted out hard, full, and ready.

He opened the clear glass door and came into the oversized shower stall. He loomed over me, placing his hands on either side of my shoulders. My breasts tightened up, and my sex started pulsing.

"I thought you already showered," I said, not intimidated by him in the least, my voice husky.

He smiled and let the spray cascade over his head as he leaned in to kiss me. He tasted vaguely of coffee as he slipped his tongue inside my mouth. A moment later his hands were on my breasts, lifting and massaging, brushing his thumbs back and forth over my sensitive nipples.

"Alec," I sighed, running my hands over his chest, gliding through the water rivulets. I tweaked at his nipples as he pulled at mine. He jumped a little. I became bolder, slicking over his ribs until I had him in my hand, stroking his length, and cupping his heavy sac. The power I had over him was intoxicating, but I was still unsure. I didn't want to go too far.

I didn't have to worry for long as he lifted me against the wall and slid inside me. I was sore, but I still wanted him there. He fit me perfectly, as if he belonged there. His hips ground into me, driving me higher, filling me. The cool tiles against my back, the warm water cascading around us, and the hard, hot man inside me was too much. I came hard with his name on my lips.

He kept pushing in and out of my body. When his grip on

me tightened, I knew he was close. He jerked out of me and sprayed across my stomach, his cock pulsing with each jet.

We rested for a moment, breathing hard.

"Good morning to you too!" I declared, grinning up at him. He laughed his grunting laugh, and I couldn't help but think this was mine. Just mine.

He washed my hair, digging his fingers into my scalp. I let him do it, enjoying every minute. He spread conditioner and combed it through, stroking the length. He took my bath puff and washed my body, paying special attention to my breasts and legs. I let him do that too. The water started growing cold and both of us were getting pruney before he got us out and dried us off with the somewhat damp towel. He insisted on wrapping us up in the comforter and getting on the bed, even though my hair was still wet. He laid me on my back, curled next to me. His arms wrapped around me, and those feelings of safety and security did too.

This was foreign to me. Even though I was warm and safe in his arms, I was still unsure and scared. I knew he wouldn't hurt me physically. Club members protected women and children, no matter what. Even the club women like Donna and Nikki were safe here. What I was scared of was whether I would get too used to this feeling and it would be ripped from me. Mute had done a complete switch from the gruff and growling badass biker to this wonderful, giving, gentle lover, and I was having a hard time figuring out which one was real.

I'd not taken a lot of chances in my life. I'd seen a lot of people get hurt taking risks. Broken spirits, broken hearts, and broken bodies littered those pathways, and I had never wanted that to be me. My foster families took care of me, but I was still always the foster kid, the extra that could be removed if needed. If I ever started to care about those people, I would get hurt when I was moved to a different home and the process began again. Millie was the only one who really took a chance on me. When the social worker came to take me away, she told me that as long as she was alive I had a home to come to no matter what. Did I have that again, here with this club? Here with Mute? Could I risk my heart again?

Mute shifted, picked up his phone from the nightstand and began typing, angling the device so I could watch the words appear on the bright screen.

Mute: Whats wrong?

I hadn't realized that I had started crying. Big tears were flowing from my eyes, almost blinding me.

"Nothing, I'm good. I'll be okay in a minute." My voice quavered.

Mute: Whats making you cry? Talk to me.

"I'm just.... I'll be fine." I brushed away the moisture on my face and tried holding my breath to keep it in.

Mute: Talk to me Kat

"Mute, I'm good." My breath hitched, and I fought harder.

Mute: In this room I'm Alec. Talk to me.

"Please, Alec, I'll be fine." I wasn't fine. I was losing it.

Mute: Baby talk to me. Please.

I didn't know if it was the "baby" or the "please" that

did it, but the dam burst. I let loose, and with a strangled cry, I buried my face against his chest. All the emotions I'd been holding back for months came out in huge sobs. I couldn't hold it back any longer. Alec held me the entire time, brushing soft kisses against my still-wet head.

When the deluge subsided, he handed me a tissue to wipe my face and streaming nose. I flushed with embarrassment at the mess I left across his chest, and wiped him up as well.

"I'm sorry. I don't do this a lot." I waved a hand at my face.

Mute: I know. Its ok. Talk to me.

I hesitated. His eyes were earnest, his caressing hands warm.

"I'm scared," I blurted. "Not just scared, I'm terrified. So much has happened. The club. Betsey's bar. Us." My voice faded. "I don't know how to handle it all, and I don't want anyone to get hurt." *Especially me*, I silently added.

Mute: We dont need to figure it out today. A lot is happening with the club and with us. Let it lie for now and we can deal when we need to. Betsey needs a lot for awhile so dont worry about work. got plenty of that shit.

I nodded, good for the moment. This was not much different than the way I dealt with most messes in my life. I got through them and survived. If it all disappeared tomorrow, I would still be breathing. Sad and hurt, but breathing.

Mute: don't cry no more.

When we entered the main room, a few people applauded. I flushed from head to toe, both in embarrassment and in wariness. A quick look at the man standing beside me told me he was no longer the sweet, considerate Alec I'd met back in the bedroom. He was back to being rigid sergeant at arms Mute. Did that also mean he was going to start treating me like a pariah in public again?

He dispelled that thought by pulling my neck back and kissing me thoroughly in front of everyone. I heard the room fill with catcalls, whistles, and more applause as Mute filled my mouth with his tongue. There was no doubt to anyone he had staked his claim on me. I was now officially Mute's old lady.

My body started pulsing with need, and I was shocked that I could still want more even after a very full night and morning of intimacy. Mute let me go, and gestured to the kitchen where Betsey and Tambre were working.

"Go help. Betsey needs you. I got stuff to do. Text later about plans."

I smiled, thinking perhaps I could find work as a mind reader. Mute frowned, and I almost giggled as he tried to slip back into his Mute persona. It wouldn't help his super tough guy image to have me laughing at his familiar scowl.

Betsey was pulling two oblong glass baking dishes filled with steaming breakfast casseroles from the oven, and Tambre was icing several more filled with fresh warm cinnamon rolls. Donna was loading the massive dishwasher with the breakfast dishes the kids had produced.

"I don't see why we can't use paper plates," Donna was complaining when I walked in. She froze when she saw me, imitating a deer in the headlights.

Betsey sighed and explained in an aggravated voice, "For

the umpteenth time, the trash cans are already overflowing. A group this size could fill them up twice over with garbage, and we ain't got no big dumpster up here. Garbage truck can't make it up the hill, and I ain't gonna have a club dumpster at the road entrance. Looks tacky! Cain't make no pile a bags 'cause we got 'coons out there that would get into 'em and make a bigger mess. I gotta take the trash down in the utility truck to the bar dumpster to get rid of it, and I ain't spending any more time on that than I have to."

She paused, her eyes growing moist. "Prob'ly all that's left of my bar is that dumpster. I hope it's still there."

I felt my nose tingle in response to her grief, but it was time to break the tension, and I knew just how to do it.

"Morning, Betsey. Looks like I missed the first rush. What can I do to help?"

The older woman's face lit up and her tears vanished. She put the fragrant baking dishes on the stove and hugged me, her arms still encased in elbow-length oven mitts. "Woo-hoo, girlfriend! 'Bout damn time you showed up. I was wondering when Mute was gonna let you up for some air! Good for you! Been waiting a sow's age for that boy to settle down."

Donna was not happy at Betsey's exuberance, and Betsey paid no attention to her. She finished loading the dishwasher and left, not bothering to wipe the counters.

Betsey started rattling off random thoughts and plans, her grief forgotten for the moment. "Brick already told me the lockdown will be a soft one since we got people that still have to get families and get up here. Once they do, the compound will get shut down tight at night and no entrance from anyone we don't know, probably till sometime tomorrow night but maybe longer. Supplies gotta get figured out before then. Brick'll keep it that way for a few days or until the fire chief confirms what happened. I gotta sit down with Stud and Mute and go over the bar accounts. Stud says he keeps records in something called a cloud. Don't know what all that mess is, but Stud knows all 'bout that internet stuff!"

I started wiping the counters that Donna had left. Betsey continued. "I'm glad he's doing the books. If I had all the paperwork stored at the bar, we'd be in a heap of trouble now! Kat, you kept the inventory records with Stud 'bout the bar, right?

I nodded and said yes at the same time.

"Good, good. One less hurdle to deal with. Gotta call the insurance guy today. Brick or Stud may have already done it, but I'd best check behind them. I'm gonna need you, Kat, to do more around here if you can. Jonelle's in rehab again, damn that woman! I gotta keep my grandkids after school every day now for the next six weeks. Maybe longer. I'll have them here for most of the time, but not on a nightly basis. Homework, school projects, and now Shells is talking 'bout gymnastics or tumblin' or dancin' or some such. Lord have mercy! I'm about to bust wide open!"

She grabbed her back and stretched. I could hear the popping from across the room. "That's it, I'm done. Tambre, will you go tell the boys this is the last set of breakfast casseroles I'm makin' today? Come get it or fend for yourself! Me and Kat's gonna have us a sit down."

I poured two cups of coffee and added the cream and Splenda I knew Betsey preferred. We settled at a corner bistro table. Betsey sighed loudly as she sat down.

"Ohhh, that's good! I've been on my feet so long this morning I forgot my knees bent this way!"

A twinge of guilt hit me as I remembered what I was doing this morning when I could have been helping the older woman.

"I'm sorry I wasn't here earlier, Betsey. If you need me, all you have to ever do is ask and I'll be there."

"No, no, darlin', you were exactly where you needed to be. I been waitin' a long time for this. Mute's a good man and needs a good woman. Not just needs one, he deserves one."

She leaned back in her chair and I prepared for a wealth of Betsey knowledge.

"I watched most of these here boys grow up, and they feel like my own. When they hurt, I hurt, and when they're good, I'm good. Mute's mama was not a good person. She was a drunk, and a mean one. She gave it a real go and did real good when he was a baby, took motherhood serious for a while, but the drink called her back. First time I seen him as a boy, he was wearin' raggy clothes that didn't fit him, and he was hungry. Lord have mercy! There's nothin' worse in this world than lookin' at a hungry child. He started comin' home with Blue after kindergarten, and kept comin' all through school. I fed him and helped him and it would 'bout kill me that he still had to go home to her every night.

"Lord only knows what he seen as a child. He grew up angry at the world, and I do mean angry! Used to pick fights at school, mouth off at teachers, make as much trouble as he could. I took him to the doctor to get him stitched up more than once from a fight. Through all that mess, he was always good to me, good to the club. Brick and me wanted to bring him home, but legally he wasn't ours, and too young to prospect at that time. I wanted to bring in CPS, you know, Child Protective Services, but he didn't want that. I think he wanted to be in our family whether it was just us or the club family, but he always felt unworthy, like he was dirty or somethin'.

"The minute he turned eighteen, he was out of here. Moved to Atlanta. Brick and me didn't hear from him for over a year, until the hospital down there called about his throat. I did what I always do for one of my boys. I got in the truck and I brought my boy home. I still remember looking at him in that bed, all sorts of tubes and needles and beeping machines. He was awake and he knew what had happened to him. He knew he would never talk again, but he was alive and by the hair on Jehovah's balls, he was coming home!"

Betsey's voice broke as she shared about Mute, just as much her son as Blue. The fierceness of this woman for her family was amazing.

"He's been here ever since. Mute's one of the most loyal brothers in the club. He loves long and he loves hard and he loves complete, but he don't love easy. I always said when he falls, it will only be once, and the woman that finally gets him will have his total devotion. He'll spend every minute of the rest of his life to give her the world and make her happy. I ain't never seen him like this with any other woman, Kat. That Maya girl messed with his head and his heart, but he never felt for her what he feels for you. I think he's fallen and fallen all the way. I think you have too, but please have a care with my boy."

I couldn't help myself. I got up and hugged her.

"No matter what he says or does, Kat, he's a good man," she whispered. "Please give him a chance."

I didn't get a chance to reply, as the kitchen was suddenly filled with more hungry kids' mouths.

"Lord have mercy, children! Stop acting like a pack of wolves and get in a line! There's plenty for everyone." Betsey barked out orders like an army drill sergeant, and I laughed at them snapping straight and lining up. She so lied. She would make more casseroles if they were needed.

CHAPTER THIRTEEN

I spent the rest of the day puttering around the lodge, helping to entertain the kids and controlling the mess that so many people inevitably left no matter how neat they tried to be. Mackie was having a ball, telling more war stories and playing with the kids. They tried to teach him how to work the video game controls, but with one hand it was pretty hard. One of the older kids held it down on a table while Mackie worked the multidirection buttons like a joystick. His neck twitched, but his hand barely trembled. They were playing the ever-popular racing game Mario Kart, and the main room was filled with kids screaming encouragement and Mackie's creative cursing.

"Dagnabbit! Get back on the road you sh— turkey-head! Son of a b—ah, broccoli eater!"

Betsey and I prepped and put out trays of cold cuts, breads, raw veggies, and a big bowl of chips. People just helped themselves when they wanted something.

The club men wandered in and out. There was another

church meeting in the late afternoon. Mute came in just before it started, seeking me out first and enveloping me in his heavy, warm embrace before tromping upstairs.

"You hungry? I'll fix you a sandwich if you want?" I muttered from within his tight hold, my own arms circling his waist.

He shook his head and flipped his fingers.

"Later."

Later meant much later. The sun made its way over the horizon, and most of the families retired to cabins for one more night, as so many people felt safer staying here for the time being. Mackie wandered off to his room, obviously exhausted from the day but glowing with happiness. This soft lockdown situation, despite the reason, was good for him. One of the kids had dubbed him "Big Daddy Mack," and he declared someone had to get him a sweatshirt with his new moniker on it.

I went back to Mute's room and stripped, putting on one of Mute's worn black tees. I curled up on the bed and took out my laptop with the intention of getting some studying done. I had one more week until my final semester started, and I was set to do more hours at the hospital. The head nurse was already saying I would have a full-time job when I graduated if I could keep up my GPA, and the new internship would have some paid hours as well. Since moving in with Mackie had cut my expenses down to practically nothing, the loss of the bar job wouldn't affect me too much financially, but I didn't know how it would affect Betsey and the club. Brick seemed to have things in hand though, and the overall feeling I got from both of them was that the club was good with money and it would survive.

I ended up falling asleep, and woke up when the door opened. Through bleary eyes, I looked up to see Mute standing in the doorway. No, it wasn't Mute, it was Alec. I could tell by the way he gazed at me. His look was softer and more intimate than when he was Mute.

He also looked uncertain, like something was weighing heavily on him. He had a sheaf of yellow legal pad papers in his hand. He handed them to me, and went into the bathroom, taking off his shirt as he went and tossing it toward the chair. I heard the shower turn on.

The sheaf of papers was indeed torn from a legal pad, a handwritten letter from Mute.

Dear Kat,

I wrote this today for you. I hope when you read it you really know what I'm trying to say. I am scared that when you know me more, you will leave but I hope you dont. I still have to be honnest with you. You are the kind of woman who needs that and I feel I have to be that way for you.

I'm not a good man. I've done bad things and I've hurt people. I'm not a smart man. I only finished high school, mostly because Betsey and Brick made me. I'm an alcoholik. I grew up with one and became one. I dont do those meetings you hear about. I just don't drink anymore. You already seen what happens when I do. I know bikes and bars and I know how to enforce. I dont date. I dont do flowers or candy or romantic dinners or walks on the beach in the moonlight or shit like that. I dont know how. What I do know is you get what you see. Nothing else. My needs are simple and I like it like that. I been on this earth for thirty-six years and I dont mean to change.

I done tried to stay away from you. I done tried to ignore you. I done tried to make you feel bad. I done tried every which way I can think of to push you away, but I cant no more. I know you think your invisible cause you said so. I seen you try to stay out of the light but yours shines too bright. When I'm with you I want to be that guy. The one who does the flowers and that other shit. I want to do more than bikes and bars and enforce. You make me feel things I got no right to feel or want. You make me into the man I should be. I dont feel this way about other women. Just you.

I want you to be in my arms when we wake up in the morning. I want to feel you beside me when we go to bed at night. I want you to ride behind me on my bike. I want to see you spread wide in my bed for me. I want you to wear my patch that your my old lady and I'm your old man just like Betsey and Brick. I'm not a good man. I dont know what love is or how it is supposed to feel. I thought I did once before but its not like it is now. I cant say it out lowd to you even if I could talk but if you can find your way to being my old lady, I'll give you all of me. Everything I am for every minute of the rest of your life.

Mute was still in the shower when I finished his letter. The grammar was rough, the spelling was creative, and punctuation was only hinted at. It must have taken him hours to write based on the amount of crossed-out lines and rewrites. Still, it was perfect.

I got out of the bed and took off the tee I was wearing and threw it on top of the one Mute had thrown on the chair earlier. I dropped my panties at the bathroom door, and walked into the steamy room. Mute was under the spray, hot water streaming down his magnificent body. He watched me as I opened the shower door and came to him. His arms came up and he crushed me fiercely into his slick body. I wrapped my arms around him as far and tight as I could. We stood like that for what seemed like a long time, just holding on to each other, keeping close enough to meld together into one person. I could feel his heart pounding as if he'd run a race. Writing a letter like that, pouring out his feelings, was not in Mute's nature, and the risk he took with me was monumental. For all his mass and badass persona, he was still able to be hurt, and only I had that power.

"I love you," I whispered into his chest as I slid to my knees. The shower was becoming one of my favorite places. It didn't matter how we went into it, we always came out clean.

I slid him into my mouth as far as I could take him, his musky taste rich on my tongue. I sucked at him, using my hand to stroke what my mouth couldn't. He leaned back with a groan and let me pleasure him at my own pace. His fingers ran through my wet hair as my head bobbed between his legs. He pulled at me, but I was determined to stay where I was, and when he came, I swallowed everything he gave me.

Later, when we were dry and in bed, he curled around me, holding me in the shelter of his body. He really didn't have to say the words, even if he could out loud. I could hear it in my head.

"I love you too."

CHAPTER FOURTEEN

I headed into the Lair, intending only to get the club ready for the members' arrival later that afternoon. The text Mute had sent was for the emergency lockdown to get solid that night, and now that I knew what that meant, I needed to help get it ready for the mass of people that would be coming soon. The building was eerily silent, and even in the daylight, it felt creepy. It wasn't very often that the lodge was empty, but with all the members either working, running escorts for errands, or chasing leads on these mystery dealers, it wasn't surprising. Betsey and Tambre were gathering children's stuff and other bits. Molly was spending her time at the sheriff's office, both for work and for information. The Lair was supposed to be the most secure of all the club holdings, but I was still glad to have Mackie with me.

"I'm gonna settle over here and see if I can catch a game or three," he grunted. He was having one of his good days, but still the stress of all that was happening showed on his craggy face.

"No problem, Mackie. Want anything? I need to take stock of the kitchen as well as the booze and text Betsey before she finishes up at Costco. Brick thinks it's gonna be another full weekend, and you know how Betsey is."

Mackie let out a half groan, half laugh as he plonked himself on one of the plush couches.

"Yep, I do. She'll have a right nice hissy fit if there ain't enough toilet paper. I tell ya, roomie, I cain't wait until Mute or whoever catches them sumbitches. I'm gettin' tired of them messin' with my people. Grab me a couple cold ones before you start doing stuff, would ya?"

"What'll it be?" I grinned at our inside joke.

"Mix 'em!" he declared, laughing again and clicking the big TV to ESPN.

I brought him the first two cold bottles my hands hit from the cooler, kissed his grizzled cheek, and went to the back storage rooms to count toilet paper rolls and take stock of other needs.

I was halfway through the second set of shelves when I heard an angry yell and thump. My first thought was Mackie was cursing at the TV, but then I heard high-pitched laughter, and my heart stopped. I ran down the hallway into the main room and froze in horror. Mackie was laid out on the floor, blood streaming from a cut on his head. Joker was standing over him, laughing and dancing around. Box was with him, a baseball bat in his hand.

I cried out, and not even considering the danger I was in, I rushed to Mackie's side, automatically feeling for a pulse and checking his other vitals.

Joker stopped laughing.

"Well, well, well! Lookie here, Box. I thought we would find the queen, but instead we got the pussy!" he said in his singsong voice.

"What have you done?" I yelled, putting what pressure I dared on Mackie's head wound. They tended to bleed a lot anyway, but a blow from a baseball bat could be fatal, especially to someone with Mackie's condition.

"Supposed to get the queen," Box said confusedly. "Queen's supposed to be here." He'd never impressed me with his powerful brain.

Joker giggled. "Nope. No queen today, but this is still good! We got the newest club princess, Mute's ol' lady. We'll take her instead, it will still have the same effect, but better for me!"

He jerked my head back by my hair, and I cried out from the pain.

"I'm gonna fuck Mute's little Pussy Kat. I'm gonna fuck it raw and when I'm done, I'm gonna hand it over to the rest of the gang to fuck. When they get done, I'm gonna fuck its ass!"

Box scratched his head and a small shower of dandruff floated to his shoulders. "But I thought Prez wanted the queen?"

Joker's hand tightened in my hair. He was clearly irritated with Box's dim mind. I whimpered, but he didn't loosen his grip.

"Prez don't know a thing about this, you moron! This was my idea! My call to make. Betsey-the-queen would've been good, but this one is better. I get to make the Dragons suffer, but especially that dumb freak, Mute! Taking his woman will just about kill the bastard!" He chortled gleefully.

I looked at Mackie, still out on the floor. The blood flow had slowed, but not stopped completely. "Please, Joker! Let me take care of Mackie. He's sick and he needs help."

Joker giggled. That's right, he giggled in a high-pitched horror movie voice. "Aww! Ain't that sweet, Box? The pussy Kat wants to play nursie-nursie to a dried up old man. Sorry, bitch! Ain't happening!"

"Why are you doing this? These men are your brothers!" I gasped in a desperate attempt to reason with him.

"Brothers? You stupid cunt! These assholes were never brothers of mine! They betrayed my father! Now they are going to pay!"

I had only a moment before a fist came flying at my face, and then I knew nothing.

CHAPTER FIFTEEN

Mute pushed the skinny man up against the rough wall of the alley and tried hard not to breathe in the toxic fumes he was panting. His eyes were wild, pupils dilated from the poison he'd put in his body. It was easy to tell his preference by the nasty color of his gums and blackening teeth. Brick and Dodge, a newly patched-in member, watched as Mute held the panicked meth head.

"Where did you get it and who sold it to you?" Brick intoned, his voice going wintery.

The man squeaked. "I ain't got nothing! Lemme go!"

Brick got even colder. "I asked you a question. Where did you get it and who sold it to you?"

"I don't got it now! You guys testing me? I paid!"

Brick went to below freezing. "I'll ask one last time and I better have an answer. Where did you get it and who sold it to you?"

"I don't know his name, man! It was the one with the green hair! If you guys got stiffed it was him! Not me!"

Brick blinked, his hard face getting harder. "What do you mean, green hair?"

The guy with the green mohawk, man! He's the one with the shit! I gave the money to him."

All three Dragon Runners froze as the temperature dropped suddenly. Mute's eyes all but glittered with barely contained rage. Dodge looked to Brick, his mouth tight.

Brick stared at the junkie, his voice went low and icy. "Are you telling me you bought that crap from a guy wearing a Dragon Runner cut?"

"Yeah, man!" The addict's eyes darted around dizzyingly. "The dude with the green hair. He was with some other guy. Different logo, you know, but they was hangin' out. I heard 'em talk about blowin' up a building an' they was laughin' bout it. Said they had a plan. I paid 'em what they asked for! I didn't stiff ya!"

Dodge spoke in shock. "Joker's a traitor."

Brick's voice went arctic. "What did the other sign look like?"

"Huh?"

Brick lost all patience and roared. *"What did the sign look like!"*

The junkie squeaked and tried to shrink into the wall. "It was kinda like yours but had a weird-lookin' horse's head."

Dodge inhaled sharply. "It's the Dead Horsemen, all right. I understand they been wantin' to take over the Tail for decades. This is them trying again and getting dirty about it by putting drugs in our town. That's the one thing they know would start a war. Leaves one club in charge and one club dead."

His phone rang, and he paused to answer it.

Mute ground his teeth, itching to smash something. It was mind shattering. Despite the differences he had with Joker, the thought of the smiling, laughing man, always sure of his welcome into the Lair, coming among those he called brothers only to betray them in the worst possible way, was more than he could stand. His hand clenched around the junkie's throat, wanting desperately to crush it. The man squeaked again at the sudden pressure, and clawed at the thick fingers surrounding his thin neck.

"Ease back, brother. I think we got other business to take care of, mainly finding that motherfucker," Dodge said on a growl. He turned to Brick. "We gotta get to the clubhouse, boss. Tambre's been trying to reach us but your phone's either dead or on silent. Mackie's been hurt and Kat's missing. Mackie got walloped good but he's awake and able to talk. Says it was Joker and his buddy Box that done it."

Mute felt the rage build in him. His beautiful Kat. His old lady. Someone touched her. Someone hurt her. Someone hurt Mackie. He couldn't contain it. He jerked the struggling man from the wall and hurled him to the ground. He stood, his head back, fists raised and clenched tight. His mouth opened and a blast roared from his mangled throat, inhuman and demonic in its power.

Dodge took several steps back, his eyes wide with sudden fear.

Brick was silent as Mute let loose, the terrible cry

echoing around them. The stillness of the club president's stance was even more terrifying than Mute's white-hot rage. Something was uncoiling, readying to strike. The laughing man who played Santa Claus for children not too long ago was gone. When he spoke, icicles formed from his words. "We know who did it and why. Only one choice now since they came into our house like that. Rules say we gotta take a vote, but we already know what it's gonna be. Lockdown's back on. Find the boys. All of them. Tell them the Dragon's awake and going hunting."

CHAPTER SIXTEEN

I woke up slowly and painfully to loud music and shouting. My face throbbed where Joker had hit me. I was bound and gagged, and lying on a worn-out couch that smelled of sour sweat and other things I didn't want to think about. My throat was burning with the desire to vomit. *Don't move. Don't breathe, stay invisible.* I pulled my familiar cloak around me, and glanced around without alerting anyone I was awake. I took in as much as my limited view would allow.

This was what I had expected of a motorcycle club house. Broken, mismatched furniture, beer bottles, cigarette butts, and other trash on every surface, posters that looked like they were torn centerfolds from porn magazines. The women there were nearly naked, topless and walking around in platform heels and thongs, bringing beer bottles to the men seated or standing around a pool table.

"Ha!" yelled a gray-ponytailed man who looked in serious need of a shower. "Pay up, asshole!"

"Fuck," another man said, pulling a woman up from the stool she had been sitting on. "Here, and be quick."

"Harley?" the woman asked, obviously scared.

"Shut up and bend over, bitch. The faster he's done, the faster I can get outta here. Fuck her ass, man, not her pussy. I'm gonna poke that later."

"Gimme some grease."

I watched in horror as the woman raised her micro skirt and bent over the stool. She was an old lady according to the property vest on her back, but was being used as a prize for a bet. The man who won her had dropped his pants and was coating himself in some sort of lotion. He moved behind the woman and thrust himself into her ass. I expected her to scream from pain, but all she did was grimace, either because she was used to this abuse or because screaming would get her punished. The man pumped and thrashed, grunting with every plunge into her. She gripped the uneven stool to keep it steady, her knuckles white with pressure.

Other similar activities were going on around the room. I saw one young woman barely old enough to be there giving a man old enough to be her father a blow job. There was a table full of white powder and straws. Several bikers were enjoying the bounty.

This club was nothing like the Dragon Runners. These men were low. Abusers. They didn't care about anything except getting high and screwing as many women as they wanted. The Dragon Runners held their old ladies in the highest regard, putting them and their children before all else. Even the club bunnies were taken care of and respected.

In this club, the women were truly just property.

I tried to keep still and fake being asleep. The awkward position I was lying in made that harder and harder to do, as I could feel my back and hip starting to cramp. How was I going to get out of this? The answer was, I couldn't. I had no idea where I was, let alone how to contact Mute or anyone else from the club. My phone was gone, and I was out of options. However, if I got a chance to run, I was going to take it. The last words Joker said to me were enough to convince me I needed to take my chances with anything else. I would fight. I had too much good in my life now not to try.

A body came flying through the air and crashed into the prize winner, knocking him and the woman over.

"What the fuck were you thinking, you stupid son of a bitch?"

I couldn't fake it anymore, and sat up. No one was paying attention to me. All activity had stopped, everyone turning to watch the show unfold. Joker was getting up from the floor when the older man who threw him picked him up and threw him down again.

"It was a great opportunity, Prez."

"You dumb asshole!" the man called Prez screamed. "The fuckin' plan was to push them out slowly! Make the fuckin' money we need to get some serious fuckin' hardware! Get more recruits! We ain't got the numbers or the firepower for a full-out war with anyone, especially the fuckin' Dragons! I still can't believe you thought burnin' down their fuckin' bar was a good idea, a*nd now your dumb motherfuckin' ass* *just took one of their ol' ladies?"*

Prez threw his hands up, jamming them across his sparse gray hair, and turned away from the prostrate Joker. "Fuck!" he yelled to the room in general.

No one was looking in my direction, but I didn't dare move. The room was silent and still, the only movement and sound coming from the two men.

"No, no, no, Prez, you don't get it!" Joker wheedled from the floor. "I didn't get just any old lady! I got *Mute's* old lady! Almost as good as getting Brick's cunt in here! She's a favorite of Betsey's, and they'll want her back and will pay big time for her!"

Wrong thing to say.

Prez's craggy face turned beet red.

"*Mute?* Goddammit! What the fuck were you thinkin'? They ain't gonna pay nothing! They'll be coming here to pay us in goddamn blood and bullets! And Mute? He's gonna slit your throat ear to ear and smile while he doin' it!"

He emphasized his point by kicking out a jean-clad leg and knocking over one of the tables, sending bottles and beer flying. A woman let out a small scream. I held my breath. This could go bad for me. Very, very, bad. The door was on the other side of the room, but even if I had a chance to get to it, I had no idea where I was and I doubted I could outrun any of these men. Should I speak up? Plead my case for freedom? Maybe Prez would listen and let me go to try and stop a war. He paced restlessly in front of Joker, who was now rising from the floor. A cell phone rang somewhere in the room, and someone answered it in hushed tones.

"Prez! Come on! We got fuckin' gold here! They'll do anything to get her back, make any deals we want!" He chuckled in a high pitch. "I ain't scared of the retard." He grabbed his crotch, rubbing himself obscenely. "He'll take her back even used a little. Been waitin' to fuck that stuck-up pussy a long time. She's got two holes, we can share!"

Prez stood still, his mouth opening and closing, speechless. I was even floored at the depth of Joker's insanity. He finally exploded, "*Are you out of your fuckin' mind?*"

"Prez! Whitey just called. He's down at the Deep Gap gas station and saw a posse of Dragons on bikes heading this way fast, and they's packing heavy. We got maybe ten minutes or so before they get here."

"Get out," Prez said with a calm that was both surprising and scary. "Get the fuck out of my club before I kill you myself."

It seemed Joker was finally starting to get it that the leader of this club wasn't kidding around.

"Prez... Mike... come on, man!" he wheedled. "You were gonna patch me over after we get rid of the Dragons! I'm already there, man!"

Prez sneered, "Do you really think I would ever patch a goddamn traitor into my club? Get the fuck out... NOW!"

Joker's face hardened, his eyes going icy. "Fine. I'm going and I'm taking the cunt with me."

Prez shook his head. "No you ain't, motherfucker. The bitch stays here. Thanks to your fuckup, I gotta smooth things over. Returning her intact will go a long way."

Joker didn't even flinch when he drew his gun and shot Prez in the stomach. The room turned to chaos. Women screamed and struggled to get away from the smoking gun. Men scrambled and shouted in disbelief, unsure of what to do. Prez lay on the floor, cursing and clutching at his abdomen.

My ears rang from the gunshot, and for a moment I froze, watching the blood leak between Prez's fingers.

"You're a dead man, Joker!" he growled. He coughed, and more blood came to his lips.

"Don't bet on it, motherfucker," Joker replied in a calm voice. He raised the gun again and shot the bleeding man between the eyes.

I heard more screams. The odd thought ran through my head that these tough-talking men weren't much of a club. Not one of them tried to defend their leader, and ran away from trouble instead of fighting alongside their brothers. There were enough of them there that Joker should've been overcome and subdued with ease, but the tight brotherhood I knew from the Dragon Runners just wasn't present in this pretend motorcycle club. I watched as grown men clawed and punched at each other and the women in their efforts to get out of the room. Joker strode over to me and slapped me to get my attention. The pain was sharp across my face where I was already bruised. My head snapped sideways, hard enough that I was knocked off the couch.

"Get up, cunt. We're leaving."

Joker stood over me, the gun casually hanging in his hand. I blinked at him, dazed, and struggled to rise, my numb hands making it hard.

"Hurry the fuck up, bitch!"

He grabbed my upper arm and jerked me up. I cried out in pain, the tight gag muffling the sound. He dragged me stumbling out the door and to his bike. He paused, and yelled, "Fuck!" I saw a glimmer of hope in that he couldn't have me on the bike without untying my hands, and I was already an unwilling passenger, so setting me free would allow me to fight him, as he couldn't hold the gun, guard me, and drive at the same time.

That glimmer was snuffed when he jerked me around and stomped to an older SUV. He yanked open the driver door and shoved me at the seat. I cried out again as my shin hit the frame and I almost fell.

"Get in, bitch!"

I scrambled across in the seat as he kept shoving at me to move faster. He threw himself in the driver seat and started the car. Apparently, the owner always left the keys in the ignition, probably in case he had to make a fast getaway and didn't want to take time to look for them. I felt a giggle threaten in the back of my throat at the absurd thought, and choked it back down. Now was not the time to antagonize Joker. His eyes were wide, pupils dilated, and his movements were rough and jerky. He turned to me and pointed the gun he'd used to kill Prez at my face.

"You move or breathe wrong, bitch, I will fuckin' kill you," he stated in a calm voice that was the opposite of his wild-eyed look. I could do nothing but stare. He spun the wheel and peeled out of the lot, spraying gravel until the tires grabbed the pavement of the main road. We took off like a shot. I saw a sign, and my heart dropped to my knees. We were entering the Tail.

CHAPTER SEVENTEEN

The Dragons pulled up to the Dead Horsemen clubhouse unchallenged. Shouts and curses filled the air as the enemy club members ran in and out of the house in total chaos. One member made an attempt to threaten the Dragons.

"Ride the fuck on, assholes! You're trespass—"

A single punch from Mute had the young biker laid out flat on the ground, knocked out cold.

A topless woman awkwardly ran in heels out of the clubhouse, screaming and crying hysterically.

"Oh, my God! Oh, my God!" she kept crying, even as she blindly ran into Cutter's arms. She didn't even acknowledge it was a rival club member she was clutching. "He shot him! Oh, my God!"

Brick snapped at her. "Who was shot? What the hell is going on?"

She turned to him, her eyes streaming black mascara down her blotchy face.

"It was Joker! He... he.... Oh, my God! He done shot Prez!"

Mute went still as a statue; icy rage rolled from him in waves.

Brick's jaw clenched. "Where is Joker?" he growled.

The woman stared at Mute, frozen in place. "You're him, ain't you?" she asked, her voice low and breathy with fear.

Brick grabbed her by her upper arms, shook her twice, and barked in her face. "I ain't got time to be nice, bitch. WHERE IS JOKER?"

"He... he... I.... He took off. Up that way to the Tail, I think. I know it's a back way to get on the main run."

"Did he take anyone with him? A woman?"

"I... he... I don't know! Maybe the one he brung this afternoon. I ain't seen her here before... oh, my God!"

Brick pushed her away in disgust and boldly entered the enemy clubhouse, along with Mute and Cutter. Taz and Stud followed, but stood at the open door. Two of the Horsemen were hovering over another, who was bleeding out on the floor. The other few were wandering around the room, not sure what to do. The coppery scent of blood floated in the air. One of the Horsemen spotted the invading Dragons and made a half-hearted attempt at bravado. He picked up one of the random guns on the floor and tried to threaten Brick.

"What the fuck you doing in here? Get the fuck out!"

One of the hunched over men stood up and smacked the gun out of his hand. "Put that thing down, ya dumb shit! It's over."

He was shorter than Brick and Mute, but no less commanding. Brick greeted him by name and a nod. "Bagman. I see you're left holding it again."

Bagman grunted a laugh and shook his head. His dark hair was tightly braided to his scalp, pulling his face tight, but he still looked worn out. "I've been left holding the bag for years, Brick. Looks like I gotta do it again. Prez is gone. Joker got him. I was out back and didn't see them shots but I heard 'em and saw Joker run out the house pulling the girl with him." He ran a hand over his craggy face. "I know he wears your club colors, but he was antsy to patch in here. Prez said he could if he helped push the Dragons out. Since you got out of the drug-running business, Prez had been wantin' it back bad. 'Make lotsa money,' he said. 'Just run the Tail,' he said. Dumb fuck!"

He kicked at the dead man's boot. "I told him it was a bad idea to trust a man who would betray his own brothers."

He heaved a sigh and squared his broad shoulders. Looking up at Mute, he spoke again. "Joker has your woman, and he took a back way we got hidden to the Tail in a cage. Old black Saturn Vue. He's gotta head start, but the Vue's wheels got some alignment problems. Transmission is bad too. He's gonna hafta fight it, and it'll slow him down some. He's probably high. He's a dangerous motherfucker sober, but you already know that. He's gonna be worse now. Good luck getting your woman back. I hope she stays in one piece."

Brick started shouting orders. "Taz, gather their guns. Bagman, get your boys to find a tarp or something to cover Mike up. Spike, call Blue and get his ass over here. He knows the sheriff on this side of the border and we gotta do this legal, but nothing about drug runs. As far as Blue knows, Joker shot your prez over the kidnapping. Let's move."

He turned to face Mute and Cutter. "Mute, I know you're itching to get up the Tail. Take Cutter. Stud, find a cage and follow. This may not end well, so best have a backup. Best of luck finding Kat. If you find Joker, it's time for him to go up the mountain and not come down."

Mute nodded once, his body shaking with the need to exact revenge on Joker. He strode out the door followed by Cutter and Stud. Mute's bike roared like an animal as he took off.

CHAPTER EIGHTEEN

As still as I tried to be, I couldn't hold on to anything or control my movements. My shoulder and head slammed into the door when he flew around the next curve, and I nearly fell into his lap at the one after that. He was still holding the gun in one hand on the steering wheel, as he needed both of them to control the car. I was afraid he would shoot me by mistake, as wildly as he was spinning the wheel. I pulled at the seat belt and tried to get it fastened, but it was impossible. I grabbed at the hanging handle as best I could with my bound hands, and fought to stay upright.

Even scarier was Joker's behavior. He was talking to himself, muttering and cursing as if reciting a children's poem.

"Shoot 'em up, fuck 'em up, Jo-ker man. Make 'em bleed as fast as you can."

He jerked around a hairpin turn and I felt the car slide, tires squealing in protest. I must have uttered a sound, because Joker screamed at me, spit flying from his mouth.

"Shut the fuck up!"

He spun the steering wheel again and the car lurched, making a horrible grinding noise. He kept talking. "Fuckers think they can get away with anything. Took away my old man's pride. Left him broken. Turned pussy. I'll fuckin' show them. I'll fuckin' show them all!"

We flew around another curve, leaving rubber behind. I'd been on the Tail before on the back of a bike, and knew it was only a matter of time before we would wreck. At this speed, on these curves, we'd never survive. I was going to die today. I was sure of it. I wished I could tell Mute one more time that I loved him.

"Fuck me up the ass!" Joker hissed. I risked a glance at him. His eyes were darting between the road and the rearview mirror. "Looks like pussy man has decided to show up."

I craned my neck as far as I was able and spotted a couple of motorcycles chasing us. I recognized the one in front, and my heart skipped a beat. Mute was racing toward us, twisting in and out of sight through the wild curves. He was gaining ground fast, and I prayed he wouldn't end up smeared on the road while trying to rescue me. I tried to reason with Joker, even though I knew it was futile.

"Joker, just pull over real quick and let me out. They'll stop for me, and you can get away clean."

"Fuck, goddamn fucking motherfucker!" Joker screamed, and slammed his hands against the steering wheel. I flinched, fully expecting the gun to go off in my face.

"I gotta get away. I gotta get away." His mood flipped again as he chanted in a singsong voice, "Save it for another day. Gonna make 'em all pay."

I glanced back again at Mute and the rider behind him. He wasn't close enough for me to see his face, but I could imagine it. His dark eyes burning with intensity, his jaw tight enough to crack. I closed my eyes and sent my love out to him.

We were on a long, tight curve, and inertia was pressing me hard against the door. Joker cackled. "Great idea, Pussy Kat! You get out there and stop them." He reached across my lap, opened the door, and shoved me out. I couldn't stop him. My only thought before I hit the ground was "this is going to hurt."

And it did.

I held my arms in front of my face as best as I could. I bounced and rolled along the hard asphalt, leaving behind torn clothes, skin, and blood. My head hit front and then back. I felt a rib or two break, and something in my arm popped. Or was it my leg? I couldn't tell. The pain hit me hard, and I suddenly couldn't breathe right.

I came to rest in the middle of the road, on my side. Something was choking me, filling my throat with a coppery taste. Blood, maybe? I gasped, and bright red liquid sprayed from my mouth. Had a rib punctured a lung?

The pain was incredible as I struggled for breath. I opened my eyes to see the taillights of the car spin out of control as it flew into a hairpin turn up ahead. It hit the flimsy guardrail hard, flipped over it, and disappeared from sight, taking several trees with it. I heard crash after crash as I imagined the car rolling down the mountain and the sound went on for a long time. Joker hadn't been wearing his seat belt either, and nursing school had taught me what happens to the human body as it is uncontrollably whipped around in a violently car wreck. The chances of Joker's survival were less than none.

I was dying. There was no way I was going to make it. This was the bad part about being a nurse, in that I knew I was too injured, drowning in my own blood, and the hospital was too far away. Mute drove up to me in a screeching halt. One moment later he was down on the ground next to me, his eyes blazing with concern and fear. I heard more vehicles pull up. It was getting hard to tell, as I felt myself fading. My hands were numb, and I was so cold. Tears were pouring from Mute's dark eyes, and I could hear his thoughts as he stroked my bloodied cheek with his fingers.

"Don't die, Kat! Please don't leave me! Please don't go!"

I smiled at him as best I could. "I'm sorry, baby. I love you," I whispered with the breath I had left. My vision went black; my last sight was Mute's tears.

* * *

Mute paced up and down the waiting room. He didn't like hospitals, but being a part of a biker club meant you became intimately acquainted with them. Accidents happened, sometimes little, sometimes more, but eventually, someone had to make a trip here. He stopped and breathed in the disinfectant smell in the air. Fuck! He hated that stink!

"Mute, sit down for a bit, son," Betsey called from one of the uniform chairs. Tambre was on one side, her hands flying with a set of knitting needles. The multicolored yarn had been getting steadily longer as the hours went by.

Mute blinked at it, thinking he could measure time by that scarf, or whatever it was. When they first arrived at the hospital, Kat's still body was swarmed with people shouting orders, taking vitals, putting stick patches on her chest, needles, tubes, and IV bags. The nurse that had treated Kat before wasn't on duty, but someone else who knew Kat as a nursing student recognized her.

"Oh, Lord in heaven, it's Katwoman! What happened? How did she get like this?"

Taz had driven the van to the hospital, and gave the details to her as well as taking care of the paperwork. Kat was quickly whisked away, presumably into emergency surgery. Once she had been rushed past the emergency room doors, the place got still and quiet. Brick and the some of the other brothers had stayed behind at the accident site to deal with the sheriff and the fire department. Joker was dead, but Mute wished he could go back and kill him again.

Stud had found Mackie, and had already brought him here earlier. The old man was stable, but still admitted for the night and was resting in a room. Stud had volunteered to stay with him, giving Mute the freedom to pace and worry. Betsey and Tambre had showed up and settled in like waiting room veterans, Betsey with her e-reader, and Tambre with her knitting. The brightly colored scarf was only a few rows when Tambre had arrived. Now, it was at least a foot and a half long.

"You doin' okay, Mute? Need somethin'?" Betsey looked up from her e-reader, a pair of multicolored reading glasses perched on her nose.

Mute shook his head. *I can't sit. If I sit, I'll think. If I think, I'll lose it.*

He resumed his pacing. *Damage, so much damage. So much blood. Fuck!* His thoughts exploded anyway. He had seen other people who had tangled with the Tail and lost. Ones that didn't have nearly the injuries that Kat did. Her breathing on the frantic ride to the hospital had gotten shallower and shallower, and was undetectable when they pulled up to the emergency bay. Mute was searching for a pulse when the trauma team took over.

Night had fallen. Mute, feeling the need for what privacy he could get, turned away from everyone and went over to the large windows that made up one end of the waiting room. During the day, the view through these windows would be spectacular, showing off the beauty of the Smoky Mountains. Now, in the full dark of night, only a shadow of the mountains could be seen. The sky was clear and black, full of stars. Mute spread his arms and gripped the metal frame of the window, gazing upward. The gentle sparkle was solemn and calming. The noises of the hospital faded as he watched.

Diamonds, he thought. *Diamonds in the sky. Pure beauty. Kat should have diamonds. She needs to wear mine. Every day, my Kat should have my diamonds on her. I need to get her some. I need to put my diamond on her finger. I need....* His mangled throat closed up and he nearly choked from the emotion. *I need my Kat!* His grip on the frame tightened as tears flowed freely down his face. He closed his streaming eyes to the glittering view, and for the first time in his life he prayed to a God he'd never really believed in.

I don't know if you're there. If you're real, or just something people use as an excuse. I never really got into the church thing. Never tried, but I hope you won't hold that against me. But if what they say is true and you're all about grace and mercy, please, I'm begging you, please, don't take my Kat away! She don't deserve it! She's been through enough hell in her life and don't need to die in one! I ain't a good man. I can't promise to ever be one, and I ain't gonna lie to you about it.

He lowered his head. *But what I can promise is I will do whatever it takes to make her happy, and I will always protect her and put her life before mine. I will love her with every cell in my body until the last breath I take on this earth, and if needed, I will take her place and die for her!*

He pressed his forehead against the glass. *Please, please, please, don't take my Kat away!*

"Family for Katrina Vega?" a weary voice called out. Mute heard Betsey jump up, the vinyl of the chair squeaking as she did.

"Family's right here, Doctor. How's my girl?" Betsey's voice was hoarse with fatigue and worry, but she still sounded like the strong matriarch she was.

Mute didn't turn around. He opened his eyes and looked

up once again at the perfect night sky. The glittering stars winked at him, and their serenity washed over him. He felt their light touch his face and a sense of calmness surrounded him. He relaxed his death grip on the window frame, already knowing the answer.

"She was touch and go for a bit, but she's one tough lady. She'll be fine."

The rest of the doctor's words blurred in Mute's ears. His legs buckled, and he went to his knees, hands on the floor. He was full. Too full. Loud garbled noises came from his ruined throat as he let it all out in great sobs.

"Oh, my God! Mute!" he vaguely heard Tambre say. A moment later, he felt both women's arms around him. Betsey crooned in his ear, her own voice breaking as she cried with him. "She's gonna be all right, baby, she's gonna be just fine!"

Mute stayed still, his mouth forming the words over and over again. "Thank you! Thank you! Thank you!"

CHAPTER NINETEEN

EIGHT MONTHS LATER...

Betsey slid the last of the cookies into the oven and took the mitts off her hands. She straightened, and felt her spine crack and pop as she stretched. *Lord, have mercy!* she thought. *I'm getting too old for this kinda work.* She smiled as she looked out the kitchen window. *But it's worth every Tylenol pill I gotta take later.*

Every counter in the club kitchen was covered in massive platters of food, ready to roll out when the guests started coming later that afternoon. Tambre, Molly, and some of the other club women were finishing up the decorations in the courtyard outside the Lair, and the prospects were busy setting up every folding chair and table the club owned. Brick was outside as well, helping to "supervise," as he called it when he sat and watched the two huge barrel smokers while they cooked ribs and BBQ while holding a beer in his hand.

Betsey glanced at the clear blue sky, closed her eyes,

and tilted her head back to feel the heat of the sun's rays through the glass. The early morning fog had already been burned off, so there was nothing to cover the beauty of the day. Fall colors were starting to show, dotting the mountains with bits of red and gold. The new River's Edge Bar was almost complete. The club had hired a family construction company called Pub Builders, known for their innovative designs and work on bars. An Irish family, with the father, five sons, and one feisty redheaded daughter. They had been working on the project all summer, and the new place was bigger and nicer than the old one. Life was good.

Betsey turned, slipped the mitts back on, and pulled the crisp golden cookies out of the oven. She turned off the heat and finally let the appliance rest. Molly came in the kitchen, Tambre following at a slower pace.

"Bunting is up, tables are covered, both the round ones and the serving ones. Cake delivery just called and they're gonna be here in a half hour. Weather is supposed to be good and stay that way at least for the afternoon. Probably get a shower or two this evening. Always happens this time a year," Molly announced, plopping down in the closest chair and fanning herself. "Ooh, Lord have mercy! If I didn't know any better, I'd say I'm havin' a hot flash!"

"Your boobs starting to sweat underneath?" Betsey asked with a mischievous grin. "I've got some cut-up chamois cloths I tuck up under there. Works pretty good!"

Tambre rolled her eyes and snagged a still-warm cookie. "Boob sweat ain't nothing like the night sweats. Taz still has nightmares of waking up to the bed on fire. Swears our heating bill was cut in half that winter 'cause I was hot enough to heat the whole house."

Brick walked in as Tambre said the words "boob sweat," and promptly walked back out. All three women died laughing.

Betsey wiped her eyes. "That's my rough 'n' tough old man! He can face down a mountain lion, have prospects shakin' in their boots, but anything about women's stuff, he's running away as fast as he can! I'd better get him his beer. He's gotta big role to play in a few hours."

She walked outside into the crisp air smelling deeply of the delicious scent of hickory and barbeque. She handed Brick a cold bottle and sat down in the lawn chair next to his. He grunted his thanks and leaned back, taking a long pull.

"Fine day, ain't it, darlin'," Betsey said, more as a statement than a question. "Good one to have us a wedding. I'm so happy our boy got hisself a good woman."

Brick hiccupped and burped. "Damn miracle she's alive. Damn near lost her. Woulda lost 'em both."

"You got that right, sugar," Betsey reflected solemnly. "I ain't never seen no one hurt that bad and live. Broke ribs, punctured and collapsed lung, concussion, so many scrapes and cuts... Lord have mercy! After hearing she was gonna live and then watching my boy fall to his knees, I knew they were gonna be in for the long haul. That's a kind of love that only happens in them romance books Molly reads all the time."

Brick threaded his fingers through Betsey's. "I think we

MUTE

do a pretty good job ourselves, don't we, Mama B?"

Betsey smiled, leaned over, and kissed the man she called her old man.

"Betsey!" Tambre hollered from the porch. "They're here!"

Betsey waved and leaped up out of the chair. "See you up at the house, Papa B. You're doing a fine job with them ribs." She laughed.

***

Betsey watched the multitude of guests wandering around the courtyard and worried again for the umpteenth time about whether or not there was enough BBQ. A biker club wedding was always a big celebration, and brothers from other Dragon Runners' chapters had shown up to see Mute and Kat get married. She was tempted to send a prospect out to get some ready-made from the Ingles down the road, but a sudden roaring noise cut through her thoughts.

"God A'mighty! I'm late!" she said out loud, and hurried to get to her spot.

Kat had been fine with just being an old lady, but Mute had insisted that they go the distance and she become a wife as well. *His* wife. She really didn't want all the attention, but Mute never let up and wouldn't give in until she agreed to the big wedding with all the trimmings. Betsey chuckled a bit. She had been in the hospital room when Mute stomped in the room with a fierce scowl on his face and a small velvet box. He had popped open the top, and barely let Kat glimpse the huge rock before he took her left hand and shoved it on the fourth finger. His look dared her to take it off. Kat had stared bewildered at her now-sparkling hand, and said to Mute as if answering his question, "Yes."

The roaring got louder as the club members on their bikes got closer. They were riding in a two-by-two formation, coming up the long driveway to the festooned courtyard. Club flags were flying behind the men. Mute was in the lead on his massive black Harley, dressed in a tux with biker boots. Somehow it worked on him. *Biker pageantry at its best,* Betsey thought as she watched row after row come down the wide aisle, turn, and circle back. Mute drove up to the gazebo that had been put up for the day. The pastor had arrived and was waiting there already. Stud drove up and backed his bike next to Mute's. He was standing as the best man, since Mackie had passed.

Betsey's lip quivered a little. The old man hadn't been able to fully recover from the blow Joker had dealt him, and even though he had healed up enough to go home, he was never able to move quite the same. He passed quietly in his sleep, taking a nap in his recliner. After the funeral, a letter arrived for Mute containing a copy of the old man's last will leaving everything he had to him and Kat. No one had any idea how large that estate was until they looked at the property deed and bank accounts. Mackie had been a very wealthy man. Mute had been humbled by the gift, and used a good part of it, along with the insurance money, to get the new River's Edge up and running, making it bigger and better than before.

The guests filled the rows of chairs in front of the

gazebo, now flanked by row after row of club brothers. The music was nothing more than a boom box in front of a microphone set up with outdoor speakers. The prospect in charge of it started a recording. Taz drove up with Tambre riding sidesaddle behind him, wearing a long red dress and her property of club cut. Cutter followed closely with Molly, also in red with her cut. Betsey was driven up to the gazebo by Bruiser. All three carried thick bouquets of deep red roses.

The motorcycles revved up loudly, drowning out the sounds of the wedding march as it played on the boom box. Brick drove up slowly, his bike covered in flowers and bunting, Kat sitting sideways behind him, dressed in a long plain white maxi dress with spaghetti straps at the shoulders and more flowers in her loose hair. Molly had attempted to get Kat to wear a fancy beaded and sparkly dress, but Kat won that battle and had the dress made for her. She opted not to have a veil either. She was smiling large, and tears flowed down her cheeks. Brick eased her off the back and brought her to stand in front of the gazebo. Mute dismounted from his bike and stood there, waiting. He had eyes only for her.

The ceremony went off without a hitch. Mute took his vows by nodding, and Kat said hers in a quavery but firm voice. When the time came for the rings, she picked up the plain gold band and pushed it onto Mute's left ring finger. Mute did the same with a delicate band encircled with diamonds, and then turned to get something from Stud. He held out a special-made cut with the Dragon Runners' colors, top rocker, and the words on the back, Property of

Mute. Kat lost it, tears of joy running down her face as she slipped on the cut that bound her tighter to Mute than any ring.

Betsey started clapping as Mute bent to thoroughly kiss his new bride. Deep-throated howls and yells filled the air, and bikes revved. Stud brought Mute's bike around to the front, and the entire assembly watched, yelling and clapping, while Mute drove back down the aisle with his brand-new smiling wife riding on the back, holding him close.

As the rest of the guests followed the newlyweds to the lavish reception, Brick leaned over and put his arm around a crying Betsey. She snuggled into his bulky warmth.

"Can't ask for more in this life. Riding free. Riding clean. Riding with a good woman at your back," he intoned in his rough voice.

She rolled her eyes, dashed the wetness from them, and pushed him away. "I ain't got time for your old-man philosophizin'! I gotta get up there and see to the food. No telling what them girls is up to."

He guffawed and grabbed for her ass. "They ain't gonna miss us for a bit. Let's have our own honeymoon!"

"Get off, you horny old goat!" She laughed, not able to keep up her outrage.

"Love you to pieces, Betsey," he suddenly declared, his face going serious as he looked at her.

She smiled back at him. "Love you too, Brick. Now let's go celebrate!"

BE ON THE LOOK OUT FOR BOOK 2 IN THE
DRAGON RUNNERS SERIES

WWW.HOTTREEPUBLISHING.COM/STUD

ACKNOWLEDGMENTS

Thank you so much for reading the story of Mute and Kat! I hope you enjoyed it as much as I did writing it.

There is a lot of truth to this story as some of the places are real places and some of the characters are based on real people. For instance, the Tail of the Dragon is a real road. An eleven mile stretch of route 129 and some of the curviest asphalt ever made. There are some arguments where the Tail actually starts. Some say North Carolina and some say in Tennessee, but no one argues the tension and the thrill of riding on it. Bryson City is also a real place in North Carolina and is technically nowhere near the Tail but in the world of the Dragon Runners, I brought the two places together.

Mackie is one of my favorite people in real life. He is based on my step father, who is indeed a veteran and war hero. He lost his right arm in service to his country but never let that slow him down. Even with the diagnosis of Parkinson's disease, he has remained optimistic and is as fun loving and entertaining as he has always been throughout his life. You go Papa Don!

I want to thank the people who have helped me make this dream of mine possible. Brittany Alexander is my first beta reader and really tells is like it is, even if I don't want to hear it. Big thanks to Becky Johnson, Justine Littleton, Donna Pemberton, Laura, Mandy, Liv, and all the other people at Hot Tree Publishing for giving me this chance and holding my hand through the process. You ladies rock! Big shout out to Carrie, Franci, and Randie for their support and advice. It doesn't matter if you're a fledging author or one who has written a dozen plus novels, you still need a dream team like this one behind you!

ABOUT THE AUTHOR

ML Nystrom had stories in her head since she was a child. All sorts of stories of fantasy, romance, mystery and anything else that captured her interest. A voracious reader, she's spent many hours devouring books; therefore, she found it only fitting she should write a few herself!

ML has spent most of my life as a performing musician and band instrument repair technician, but that doesn't mean she's pigeon-holed into one mold. She's been a university professor, belly dancer, craftsperson, soap maker, singer, rock band artist, jewelry maker, lifeguard, swim coach, and whatever else she felt like exploring. As one of her students said to her once, "Life's too short to ignore the opportunities." She has no intention of ever stopping... so welcome to her story world. She hopes you enjoy it!

FACEBOOK: WWW.FACEBOOK.COM/AUTHORMLNYSTROM
TWITTER: HTTPS://TWITTER.COM/ML_NYSTROM
PUBLISHER: WWW.HOTTREEPUBLISHING.COM/ML-NYSTROM

ABOUT THE PUBLISHER

Hot Tree Publishing opened its doors in 2015 with an aspiration to bring quality fiction to the world of readers. With the initial focus on romance and a wide spread of romance sub-genres, we envision opening to alternative genres in the near future.

Firmly seated in the industry as a leading editing provider to independent authors and small publishing houses, Hot Tree Publishing is the sister company to Hot Tree Editing, founded in 2012. Having established in-house editing and promotions, plus having a well-respected market presence, Hot Tree Publishing endeavors to be a leader in bringing quality stories to the world of readers.

Interested in discovering more amazing reads brought to you by Hot Tree Publishing? Head over to the website for more:

WWW.HOTTREEPUBLISHING.COM

CPSIA information can be obtained
at www.ICGtesting.com
Printed in the USA
BVHW032147080921
616424BV00006B/72